Illustrated by Rowan Clifford

PUFFIN

PUFFIN BOOKS

Published by the Penguin Group
Penguin Books Ltd, 80 Strand, London WC2R 0RL, England
Penguin Group (USA) Inc., 375 Hudson Street, New York, New York 10014, USA
Penguin Group (Canada), 90 Eglinton Avenue East, Suite 700, Toronto, Ontario, Canada M4P 2Y3
(a division of Pearson Penguin Canada Inc.)
Penguin Ireland, 25 St Stephen's Green, Dublin 2, Ireland (a division of Penguin Books Ltd)
Penguin Group (Australia), 250 Camberwell Road, Camberwell, Victoria 3124, Australia
(a division of Pearson Australia Group Pty Ltd)
Penguin Books India Pvt Ltd, 11 Community Centre, Panchsheel Park, New Delhi – 110 017, India
Penguin Group (NZ), 67 Apollo Drive, Rosedale, North Shore 0632, New Zealand
(a division of Pearson New Zealand Ltd)
Penguin Books (South Africa) (Pty) Ltd, 24 Sturdee Avenue, Rosebank, Johannesburg 2196, South Africa

Penguin Books Ltd, Registered Offices: 80 Strand, London WC2R 0RL, England

puffinbooks.com

First published 2010

007

Set in Baskerville
Made and printed in England by Clays Ltd, St Ives plc

British Library Cataloguing in Publication Data
A CIP catalogue record for this book is available from the British Library

ISBN: 978-0-141-32795-2

www.greenpenguin.co.uk

Penguin Books is committed to a sustainable future for our business, our readers and our planet. This book is made from Forest Stewardship Council™ certified paper.

This is for Adele, and for Ivor too.

One day he will need to know all about Vikings

and dinosaurs and ancient Egyptians.

I think he should be warned.

With many thanks.

Contents

1 Big Trouble

War had broken out in Rosie's bedroom. It was only a small bedroom so the noise was unbelievable. It sounded as if King Kong was running wild in a saucepan factory.

BANNGGG!

KRRUNNKKK!

SPLUDDD!

KERRANNGG-FUDD-DIDDLYSPING-ZZZUTT!

So what was going on? Who was at war? Three armies were involved. Actually, they weren't exactly armies. Armies have lots of people in them. These only had one person each.

The smallest army was six years old and called Alfie. He had plastic Roman armour on his chest and was waving a toy space-gun. He was also wearing a North American Indian chief's headdress. He looked a little odd, especially as the chief's headdress had pushed his ears right out, making him seem a bit like a charging elephant, only smaller.

The other two armies were both nine. One army was called Dylan and the other was Rosie. They were twins. Sometimes they loved each other and sometimes they hated each other. At the moment they hated each other.

KRANNNGGG! DINNGG-DINNGG!

Rosie took another swipe at Dylan's head

with her pillow, missed him by miles and sent her alarm clock flying across the room instead. Meanwhile, Alfie was shooting both of them to Utter Death with his space-gun.

'*Peeyoooooo! Peeeyoooooo!*' (Those were meant to be Utter Death Laser Rays shooting out of his gun.)

So what was this war all about? Dylan's PlayStation. Rosie had 'borrowed' it. You know what that means. She'd snaffled it when Dylan was halfway through a game. He had put it on Pause while he went to the loo and by the time he got back, there it was, gone.

'I hadn't finished!' he yelled at his sister. 'You stinking sneakbag. I was halfway through. I was on Level Three and now you've ruined it! I've never got to Level Three before and now I have to start over again.'

BLONNKK!

That was Dylan crashing back against Rosie's wardrobe as he tripped over all the pillows and the duvet cover lying on the floor.

'*Peeyooo! Peeeyoooooo!*' went Alfie, adding to the body count even though his frantically feathery headdress had slipped down over his eyes and he couldn't see where he was shooting. (He killed the curtains three times.)

'*STOP!*' That was their mother, putting her head round the door.

'But Dylan was –' began Rosie, just as Alfie started with, 'But Rosie was –'

'*STOP!*' repeated Mum. 'Look at this room. It's a disaster area. Give me that game right now and you can all tidy up and put the bed straight. After that it's bedtime.'

Alfie pushed his headdress up his forehead and swung the Utter Death space-gun in Mum's direction. '*Peee*–' he began, but Mum stopped him in his tracks by simply lifting her single Finger of Warning. (Mum's Finger of Warning was much more powerful than any space-gun known to Humans, Aliens or Alfie.)

She closed the door on them. A dark silence fell upon the three armies as they tidied up.

'Mum's ruined everything,' Dylan muttered. 'Just when we were having fun.'

'I was winning,' claimed Alfie.

'You were *so* not!' chorused the twins.

'It's too early for bed,' complained Rosie, sitting on the edge and scratching at her new pyjamas. They were a bit itchy on one sleeve. She soon discovered why. There was a small piece of paper stuck inside.

Rosie pulled it out and smoothed it flat.

These are Cosmic Pyjamas. Some people say it is not wise to wear the top half and the bottom half at the same time. Beware.

That was a bit odd. She showed the note to Dylan, who snorted.

'You wouldn't wear the bottom half without the top, would you? And you certainly wouldn't wear the top half without the bottom! Anyway, I don't see anything cosmic about them.'

'Well, I like the pictures,' Rosie said firmly. 'There are all kinds of things.'

It was true. The pyjamas were covered with little drawings. There were buildings and plants, mountains, forests, animals, people – all sorts.

Bandit came wandering in. He was the family cat and a bit of a monster. He was large, fluffy and totally ginger from his head to his bottle-

brush tail. He was also annoyingly nosy and wanted to know about everything.

Bandit leapt on to the bed and began padding about on as many people as possible. He licked their ears, stuck his tail up their noses and invited them all to admire his bottom. The invitation was ignored.

'Bandit, you are a PAIN in the PANTS!' said Dylan, struggling to look at the pictures on the cosmic pyjamas.

'I'm hungry,' announced Alfie.

'You're always hungry,' Dylan complained.

'Because you ate half my chips. You always steal my chips because you're bigger than me and horrible and you're a CHUNKY CHIP ROBBER MONSTER!' And just for good measure Alfie shot his big brother. '*Peeyow!*'

Rosie let out a little squeak. 'I think that picture moved,' she whispered.

'Which picture?' demanded Dylan. 'You're bonkers.'

'That one,' Rosie murmured with an anxious frown.

They all stared at Rosie's left knee. It was a picture of a cloud. The cloud was shrinking and growing. At the same time a little mini cloud came puffing out of the big one, only to vanish quickly.

'How can it do that?' asked Rosie, a wee bit alarmed. Pyjamas were not meant to have moving images. The three of them peered even closer. Bandit decided to take a look too. He went marching in, pushing his fat ginger body between the children. He put one paw right on top of the trembling cloud.

KERRANNGG BAM SSWIZZZ!

In a flash the children found themselves

hurtling through the air. Was it space? Was it anything at all? It was impossible to say. They seemed to be half flying, half falling, with colours of all sorts whirling around them, as if they were tumbling through a vast tunnel of light and dark. And then –

FLUBBB!

They landed.

They rolled about for a moment on the dusty ground, then picked themselves up. Bandit gave a little mew as if to say, *Er, what did I do?* Or maybe he was asking where on earth they were.

That was a good question. Were they on Earth at all? Dylan pointed at a huge cloud. It was approaching them fast, bowling along the ground. With it came the sound of non-stop thunder. The children waited, holding hands. Alfie held Bandit's tail. And then they realized what was making the cloud.

It was an army, a vast army of Vikings. Most of them were waving nasty, pointy swords. They were all yelling. And some of the Vikings seemed to be driving Second World War tanks. TANKS?!

'Run for it!' yelled Dylan. They turned tail,

took two steps in the opposite direction and stopped dead. Charging towards them from the other side was *another* army! They weren't Vikings this time. It was a rampaging army of ancient Egyptians. They were brandishing nasty, pointy spears and firing off arrows. And many of the ancient Egyptians were riding in chariots, pulled by galloping dinosaurs. DINOSAURS?!

'What's happening?!' screamed Rosie. 'It must be a nightmare!'

But it wasn't a nightmare. It was really happening.

2 Doctor *Who*?

The ground shuddered beneath them as the two howling armies thundered towards the children. The Viking tanks were firing at everything they saw, including themselves. The dinosaurs were charging around in circles, mostly out of control, screeching and wheezing, bellowing and yelling. The noise rose to a deafening roar. Bandit's frightened fur was sticking up so straight he looked like a giant ginger hedgehog.

'What do we do?' yelled Rosie.

'I don't know!' Dylan yelled back.

'I want to go home!' cried Alfie.

'!!!' squeaked Bandit.

The sand and earth at their feet danced and swirled as a huge, flattening wind came slapping down from above.

SHOOOOFFF!

They looked up through the dust and were astonished to see a small spacecraft slowly descending. Landing gear sprang out from the sides as it set down right next to the children. A hatchway hissed open and a metal ladder unrolled to the ground.

A voice boomed from the spacecraft. 'Get in! Quickly!'

The children scuttled up the ladder and practically fell into the machine. A moment later they were whisked up into the sky.

Alfie was hugely impressed. 'We're in a real space ship!' he breathed, his eyes like shiny planets.

Dylan sighed with relief. 'That was close.' He and Rosie stared down from the window and watched as the two armies collided and locked together in battle, raising even more clouds of dust.

A rather cross voice piped up behind them. 'Fighting, fighting. Why do humans spend so much time fighting?'

They turned and found themselves gazing up at a tall and ancient man. He was so tall he had to stoop to stop his head banging against the ceiling of the little spacecraft. He was as thin as a wisp of grass, with a poky nose, popping eyes and a tiny round mouth that looked as if it had been stolen from a goldfish. His extraordinary hair stuck out round the sides of his head, giving the impression that if you ever needed a chimney sweep's brush, he would do the job very well.

'Well, who are you?' rasped the old man and, without waiting for an answer, he went straight on. 'I'm Boctor Starkly-Donkers. I mean Stocktor Darkly-Conkers. No, no! *No*!' The man shook his head hard, slapped both cheeks and finally managed to say, '*Doctor Starkly-Bonkers*. *Yes!* That's it! Doctor-um dum-di-dum, just like I said a moment ago.'

Rosie chewed her lip for a second and then

asked, 'Could we just call you Doctor?'

'Aha-ha-ha, yes! Excellent idea.' The doctor's bulging eyes fixed on Bandit. 'You've got a cat,' he declared. 'I like bats. I mean rats. Hats. Mats. Gnats. What you're holding,' he eventually decided.

'Are you really a doctor?' asked Rosie.

'No, not at all. I just call myself a doctor because it's easier to remember than that other word.'

'What other word?' asked Dylan.

'I don't know,' admitted the doctor gruffly. 'I keep forgetting it. I think it begins with a B. No, a G. T? C? V? It's like "doctor", but longer.'

The spaceship went silent for a few seconds as everyone on board tried to think of something longer than 'doctor' that began with a B. Or a G. Or maybe a T, C or V. They all failed.

'So,' the doctor said at last. 'Do tell me who you are.'

'I'm Alfie and she's a girl and he's poo-pants,' Alfie declared.

The doctor's eyes widened and for a moment he didn't know what to say, so he hastily went on with a little nod. 'I found you, then.'

'Were you looking for us?' asked Dylan.

'Um, well now, I was certainly looking for something, only I don't know what it was, but you might be it. Things don't happen unless they are meant to happen, you know.'

Dylan pricked up his ears. 'So can you explain what's happening down there?' he asked, pointing out of the little window. 'There are Vikings in tanks and ancient Egyptians riding in chariots pulled by dinosaurs, but that's stupid because they didn't live at the same time. It's like history is all muddled up.'

'Exactly,' cried the doctor. 'You're very clever.'

Dylan beamed and turned on his twin sister. 'See? He said I'm brilliant.' Dylan tapped his chest proudly.

Rosie grunted and folded her arms. 'Anyone could have said history is muddled up. You're not *that* brilliant.'

'Maybe, but the doctor didn't say *you* were brilliant, did he? He said *I* am, and he should know because he's a doctor.'

'Flopresser, I mean professor,' said the doctor. 'That's the word I can't remember. Professor!'

'We'll stick to doctor,' murmured Rosie, who already found it difficult to follow what the doctor was saying without throwing in any more word problems.

Bandit gave a large miaow and pawed Alfie's leg. 'Bandit says he's hungry,' said Alfie. 'And I am too. Have you got any chocolate? Or rice pudding?'

'Ignore him,' muttered Dylan. 'He's always hungry, and so is the cat. You still haven't explained what's happening.'

'No, I haven't. It's the Boomduster. I mean Doombuster. The Doombuster is the ultimate weapon. It can destroy whole planets. It works on the idea of reversing an atomic split.' Doctor

Starkly-Bonkers waggled his eyebrows to show that reversing an atomic split (whatever *that* meant) was terribly important.

'Never heard of such a thing,' said Dylan.

'That's because I invented it,' the doctor declared with great pride.

Rosie was horrified. 'You mean to say you actually *made* the most powerful weapon in history – one that can destroy whole planets? That's terrible! How could you do it?'

'Ah, well, you see, I wasn't trying to make a weapon,' the doctor said hastily. 'I was trying to build a new vacuum cleaner. I gave my grandson a birthday party and it turned into a food fight. My old vacuum cleaner broke down trying to clean up the mess and I thought I had an excellent idea for a really good new one. I could use the power created by reversing the atomic split to produce a machine with greater suction.

'But the first time I switched it on it created an explosion so massive it disturbed Tace and

Spime. I mean Space and Time. That's what caused this mix-up on the planet below. The whole of history has been muddled together. Just before I came here to get you, I flew over the ocean and there was the *Titanic* steaming along, and sailing after it was a Roman warship. Incredible. Such a mess! Now I am trying to put it right.'

'Good,' declared Rosie, who was very pleased to hear it. She didn't like the sound of the Doombuster at all. 'So I imagine you are trying to mend the

Doombuster and make it into a proper vacuum cleaner?'

The doctor shook his head and looked uneasily round the room, as if he was suddenly feeling rather guilty about something. Which he was.

'Unfortunately, I don't know where the Doombuster is,' he admitted.

Rosie turned white from head to toe and back up to her head again. 'You mean to say you have invented a weapon that can destroy worlds and YOU'VE LOST IT?'

'It got stolen by pirates.' That was the doctor's excuse. 'They sold it to Julius Caesar, but then Robin Hood snaffled it from him. He was caught by the Vikings and then it went somewhere else and now I'm not sure where it is. The ancient Egyptians might have it. Or even Veen Quicktoria. I mean Queen Victoria.'

Rosie and Dylan stared at each other. This was terrifying. Someone, somewhere, had a weapon that could destroy whole planets, but nobody knew who, or where, it was.

'The good thing is that nobody knows how to use it, except me,' the doctor offered as a ray of hope.

'Is it difficult to use?' asked Dylan.

'You do have to plug it in and switch it on,' the doctor told them.

'But anyone could do that!' Dylan gasped.

'The switch is hard to find and it's a bit stiff,' said the doctor. 'It's not my fault pirates stole it. Anyhow, the thing is, everyone is after it and they're after me too. They want me to show them how it works so they can destroy their enemies. That's why I am so pleased to see you two. I mean three. No, four . . . if you count the cat.'

'Miaow,' muttered Bandit, who definitely wanted to be counted.

Rosie was puzzled. 'Why us? What can we do?'

The doctor's face broke into a broad smile and he laughed dismissively. 'Well, if you haven't been sent here deliberately to find the Doombuster, then my name's not Doctor Bonkly-Starkers. Which it isn't. I've got it wrong again, haven't I? I mean Doctor Stonkly-Bonkly. Binkly-Stinky. Stinkly-Wonkers. Starkly-Bonkers! That's it!'

Rosie and Dylan weren't listening. They were too busy taking in what the doctor had just told them. He was expecting *them* to find the world's most dangerous weapon. They would have to go back to the warring planet, right in the middle of the Vikings, the ancient Egyptians *and* the dinosaurs. THEY COULD BE KILLED!

Little Alfie stroked Bandit and smiled. 'It's going to be brilliant!' he breathed happily.

3 A Lot of Beards and One Sore Bottom

'Have you got any cola?' asked Alfie. He was very disappointed when the doctor said there was no cola on board and he would have to make do with a few peanuts and a cup of coffee. Alfie reckoned it wasn't much use having your own spaceship if you couldn't even get something decent to eat or drink.

'We went to Italy with Mum and Dad,' he told the doctor. 'On a plane, and they gave us crisps and a BIG meal on a tray AND cola. I had two lots.'

'Cola's not very good for you,' said the doctor, which prompted Alfie to say that the doctor was 'as bad as Mum'.

'Have another peanut,' suggested the doctor.

Alfie shot him a very dark look and took three peanuts because they looked so tiny. 'It's not enough for an ant,' he muttered. 'Not even a baby ant. Not even a baby ant's baby. Not even a baby ant's baby's baby.'

'Alfie,' snapped Dylan, 'zip it! You're beginning to sound like the doctor.'

Doctor Starkly-Bonkers stiffened. 'I'm not six!' he complained childishly.

Bandit wasn't interested in peanuts either. He wandered off to see if he could find something bigger, more chewy, and, hopefully, with four legs and a tail so he could chase it around a bit. It might even come in the shape of a mouse, if he was lucky.

In the meantime, Rosie had been doing some thinking. It was all very well for the doctor to claim that the children must have been sent there to help him, but they had only just escaped from deadly danger – and now he was suggesting they should go back into the thick of it. She decided to point this out to him.

'Ah! But I have the answer,' the doctor beamed. 'I agree that it would be very silly to jump straight back into that awful ding-dong going on down there. No, no, no. It would be much better to start with something a lot safer. I think we should go and join the Vikings.'

'Should we?' Rosie answered weakly. She could remember the Vikings charging towards her. They had looked very fierce and had nasty, pointy swords, not to mention the tanks.

'Surely the Vikings will spot us straight away?' Rosie suggested.

'Not at all. We shall be in disguise. It just so happens I have a whole load of costumes on board from my grandson's birthday. He had a dressing-up party – that's how the food fight started. They couldn't agree on who'd be what.' The doctor shook his head sadly. 'People – always fighting. Anyhow, the costumes could be useful. Let's take a look.'

The doctor took them to the rear of the ship and there they found a whole range of costumes – funny hats, clown gear, cowboy stuff, Viking kit, pirate clothes – all sorts.

Alfie pounced on some Roman armour. 'It's the same as mine, only even better. Wow!'

'When you're trying to sort out history, it's useful to have the right clothes,' the doctor explained, pulling out some Viking jackets and leggings. Rosie's cosmic pyjamas still showed here and there, but it was the best she could do. As a final touch, the doctor produced several false beards.

The children fell about laughing at each other. Rosie had a great fat ginger beard. Dylan's was a full black one with lots of pointy tufts. Alfie's face had completely vanished behind the whopper he had chosen.

'Pull it down under your nose, drain-brain,' Dylan ordered.

'Drain-bottom,' sniggered Alfie. He picked up a small beard and tried to fit it round Bandit's chin. 'Look! Look! Bandit's a Viking cat!'

Bandit didn't bother to try to remove the beard. He was used to Alfie treating him like a kind of four-legged doll.

'We're not taking him with us, are we?' asked Dylan.

'Yes!' shouted Alfie. 'He has to come.'

'He'll only get us all into trouble,' Dylan grumbled. 'I mean, how many Vikings wander about with a cat?'

'He's in disguise!' Alfie yelled. 'Nobody will notice. He's got to come. You're coming, aren't you, Bandit?'

'Miaow.'

'He said "*Yes*".' Alfie claimed.

'He said "Miaow",' Dylan growled. 'Anyway, if he's coming, he can't wear a beard. It looks stupid.'

The children finally managed to stop arguing and the doctor explained that they would have to hide the spaceship. They would land near the Vikings, but out of their sight.

'The spaceship has an invisibility shield that I can turn on when we leave, so nobody will spot it.'

'They will if they bump into it,' declared

Alfie. 'They'll be walking along and suddenly – *BANG*! They'll probably get a nosebleed or knock themselves out. Then they'll know where it is. And they'll have to go to hospital and I bet their mums will be really cross with you and come round to your house and say you're a bad, bad man and you'll be in BIG trouble.'

The doctor sighed and asked the twins if there was an invisibility shield for small boys, or at least something that would stop him talking. It wasn't necessary because by that time they were about to land back on the planet. A hush fell on all of them. Their adventure was about to get even more dangerous.

With a gentle bump the spaceship made contact with the ground. The doctor checked all was clear and they clambered down the ladder. He pressed a button on the side of the spaceship and all of a sudden they couldn't see it.

Bang! Bang! Bang! The doctor tapped his finger on the side of the invisible ship. 'You see? It's

still there,' he said happily, and led the way towards the Viking camp.

'We must all pretend to be Vikings, so try to speak in a low voice,' suggested the doctor. 'We must have Viking names too. Here are some I know: Erik, Thor, Sigurd, Harald, Magnus, Ulf, Leif – take your pick. We're almost there and we've been spotted,' he finished urgently. 'Get ready to be a Viking!'

'Pull your beard down, Alfie,' whispered Rosie as they entered the Viking camp.

'What about Bandit?' asked Alfie. For a moment the others were silent, then Rosie scooped up the cat and shoved him down the front of her top.

'Stay still and don't dig your claws in,' she commanded.

The camp was hugely busy. Many of the Vikings were sharpening their swords. Others were preparing food or building shelters for the night. Some of the Vikings were polishing their tanks. Everywhere there were Vikings wandering about, looking grim and battleworn.

A trio of guards stopped the newcomers at the gate. 'Who goes there?' shouted the biggest, hairiest Viking.

'I'm Th-Th-Thief,' blurted the doctor. 'I mean Teeth, Keith, Chief, Leif – that's it! Leif Bonkersson!'

Dylan stepped forward next and growled in as

low a voice as he could manage. 'Erik the Red.'

One of the other Vikings bent down and pushed his scarred and hairy face right up close to Dylan's. 'You can't be Erik the Red,' he snarled. '*I'm* Erik the Red already!'

Dylan thought quickly. 'I mean I'm Erik the Redd-ish,' he corrected.

The other Vikings hooted with laughter. 'Erik the Radish? He said he's Erik the Radish!' Even Rosie giggled.

Dylan stamped one foot. 'Erik the REDD-ish, and don't you laugh at me, or I'll turn your brains inside out.'

'Ooooooh, we are *so* scared,' sniggered one of the three guards. 'All right, who are these others, then?'

'Sigurd the Strange,' said Rosie calmly.

'What's so strange about you?' demanded Erik the Red. Then he noticed the strange lumps and bumps moving about under Rosie's jacket.

'That's certainly peculiar,' he said. 'What's going on there?'

The doctor came to the rescue. 'She's got squirmitis.'

At that moment a ginger tail slipped out from the bottom of Rosie's jacket.

'And it's getting worse,' the doctor added as Rosie hastily pushed it back in. 'Squirmitis – horrible disease. Highly infectious.'

Erik the Red backed away and turned to Alfie instead. 'Well, titch, who are you?'

'I'm Thor,' said little Alfie. 'Thor Bottom.' It's a good thing Alfie's face was almost completely covered by his beard, otherwise the Viking guards would have spotted the huge grin underneath it.

'You're mighty small, Thor Bottom. How come you're so short?' demanded Erik the Red.

'He hasn't had any breakfast,' Dylan answered quickly.

Erik the Red frowned for a moment and then nodded. The guards parted and the little band of adventurers entered the camp proper, one of them holding her wriggling tummy and cursing Bandit under her breath as the cat kneaded her stomach with his claws.

4 A Nice, Quiet Viking Chat Round the Campfire – As If

The Vikings were very noisy, shouting and roaring at each other, pushing and shoving and collapsing with laughter when someone fell over, as if it was the funniest thing in the world.

'It's like the playground at school,' Rosie remarked tartly. 'Only worse.'

'Keep your eyes open for the Boomduster, Broom-mustard, I mean Doomfluster. Oh, you know! The Thingy!'

'I take it you mean the weapon that can destroy planets?' Rosie still hadn't forgiven the doctor for creating such a monstrous thing in the first place.

'I didn't know the vacuum cleaner would go so wrong,' the doctor explained. 'Besides, we have to get the Doombuster – there, I said it! – we have to get the Doombuster back for two reasons. One – we must stop anyone trying to use it to destroy things. And two – I have realized that we need the Doombuster to put everything right. There are bits and pieces in the machinery that will help me put history back in the right order.'

Dylan wanted to know what the Doombuster looked like, so they knew what to search for.

'It's long, silver, blue and red. One end looks like a very large, fat sausage. There's a long tube poking straight out of it with a wide mouth on the end. That's the bit that was meant to suck things up, only it didn't. Blew them to bits instead.'

It occurred to Rosie that maybe the doctor's big problem was that he often got things mixed up. The Doombuster was blowing instead of sucking, and he was always getting his words round the wrong way. Maybe it was a coincidence. Maybe it wasn't. Rosie decided to keep a close eye on the doctor in case he got anything else important muddled up.

The four and a half searchers, (that's four humans and a cat, but don't tell Bandit), wandered around the camp for hours. At least that's what it felt like, especially to Alfie. After all, his legs were shorter than everyone else's, apart from Bandit, of course.

'I'm hungry,' Alfie complained. Again.

'We haven't got any food,' Dylan said wearily. 'And I'm fed up.' He flung a scowl at his twin sister. 'This is all your fault. You and your stupid cosmic pyjamas.'

'I didn't know they'd bring us here,' responded Rosie. 'Besides, it was Bandit who trod on the flashing picture.'

'Huh! Don't know why you wear pyjamas anyway,' Dylan grumbled.

'Because it was bedtime, beans-for-brains!' Rosie shot back.

Doctor Starkly-Bonkers could see a major argument was brewing. It was because everyone was hungry. He pointed out a small group of Vikings sitting round a fire, barbecuing some meat. The smell of roasting drifted across and went straight up his nose, making all his taste buds tingle.

'Let's see if we can join that group of Pikings, I mean Bikers, Vipers, Vikings! They might let us share their food.'

'Brilliant!' cried Alfie, already hurrying over with Bandit in tow.

'Don't suppose they'll let us have any,' Dylan muttered grumpily.

'Ignore him,' said Rosie. 'He complains about everything.'

'I don't complain about everything,' Dylan complained. 'I only complain about *you* and one or two other things.'

'Everything,' teased Rosie.

As Dylan opened his mouth to argue, the doctor hastily broke in. 'Oh, look, they're toasting a boat. I mean posting a stoat, roasting a goat! Smells delicious. Come on, and while we're there we might find out something about the Doombuster.'

The group of diners shuffled along the logs they were sitting on, to make way for the newcomers. They introduced themselves, with Dylan telling everyone he was Erik the Redd-ish – 'That's red, the colour,' he underlined. He didn't want any more radish jokes. He was feeling grumpy enough as it was.

The Vikings were quite happy to share their meal, but they stared at Alfie and Bandit an awful lot.

'You're pretty small,' said one, who was

wearing a patch over his left eye.

'I've always been the smallest,' Alfie burbled, trying hard to produce a deep voice. It sounded as if he was talking underwater. 'I was small when I was born.'

'You should eat more meat,' nodded another Viking. 'That'll make you grow.'

'No, it's fish that makes you grow,' said the third Viking.

'Uh-uh,' grunted the fourth. 'Fish is for your brain. It's cabbage that makes you taller.'

'Meat,' repeated Patch-eye.

'Fish,' snapped the third Viking.

'Cabbage,' put in number four.

The first Viking, the one who had started it all by saying how small Alfie was, got to his feet. 'Actually,' he said, rolling his head commandingly, 'it's not meat, fish or cabbage that makes you taller.'

'What is it, then?' chorused the others, along with Alfie. They all wanted to know.

The first Viking sniffed and smiled. 'Actually, what makes you taller is a pair of stilts. Ha-haah!' And he roared with laughter while the other three fell backwards off their log, clutching their sides. They clawed their way back on to the seat. Bandit gave them a withering glance and carried on tearing at the piece of goat he'd managed to steal.

When the Vikings finally settled back down, Doctor Starkly-Bonkers tried to steer the talk round to the Doombuster.

'That's a mighty sword you have there,' the doctor told Patch-eye.

The Viking drew his sword and waved it proudly over his head. 'This is my sword Belly-Ripper,' he declared. 'With this weapon I have slain many men.'

The other Vikings wanted to show off their swords too. One by one they drew them from their leather sheaths.

'My sword is named Skull-Splitter,' said one.

'And mine is called Headache,' said another. 'Because when I hit you on the head it will give you the worst headache *ever*!'

The doctor nodded and said nice things about all the swords, but he had a more important question for the Vikings. 'What do you think the most powerful weapon in the world is?'

The Vikings looked at him sharply. Patch-eye's

good eye glinted in the flickering flames from the fire. He smiled, stroking his thick beard. 'That would have to be The Thing That Makes Planets Go SPLAT,' he declared.

The others nodded their agreement. 'The Thing That Makes Planets Go SPLAT,' they chorused quietly.

The doctor looked at Dylan and Rosie and winked. The Vikings must be talking about the Doombuster! It couldn't be anything else. Their first clue, at last.

'Have you ever seen The Thing That Makes Planets Go SPLAT?' asked Rosie.

The other Vikings looked at her in surprise. 'You've got a very girly voice,' one of them told her.

Rosie coughed and scowled before answering. 'Had a bone in my throat,' she said as gruffly as possible. 'So, have you ever seen that weapon?'

'Didn't you see it?' growled Patch-eye. 'Huh. We had it, didn't we? In our hands. It was ours.

Then those sneaky ancient Egyptians came along with their scary dinosaurs and stole it from us. Took it for themselves, they did. Now we're at war with them, trying to get it back. And we have to find the doctor as well, cos he's the only one who knows how to make it work.'

'The doctor?' Dylan prompted. 'I don't know what he looks like.'

'He's very tall – a bit like your pal there next to you. And his hair sticks out – a bit like your pal there. But he's bald on top – a bit like your pal there. In fact, he looks just like your pal there, apart from the beard.'

Dylan nudged the doctor. 'You look just like him.' He was trying to make a joke of it. They were all chuckling at the extraordinary likeness of the doctor to himself when Alfie finished eating. He gave an enormous Viking burp and wiped his greasy mouth clean with the back of his hand.

Unfortunately, before he wiped his mouth, Alfie PULLED DOWN HIS BEARD!

Instant uproar followed. The Vikings goggled at Alfie and his removable beard. Patch-eye lunged forward and yanked hard on the doctor's beard, tugging it from his chin. Then he tore at Rosie's beard, and almost died of shock when he realized she was a girl.

Before the Vikings could raise the alarm the four and a half were on their feet and racing away.

'After them!' roared Patch-eye. 'It's the doctor and *a girl*! And Erik the Radish –'

'Redd-ish!' Dylan yelled back.

'Catch them!' bellowed Patch-eye. 'They're after The Thing That Makes Planets Go SPLAT!'

The Vikings leapt up in a heaving mass and came charging after the runaways. Howls and whoops rose from every corner. Swords sliced the air threateningly. Teeth got gnashed, beards got nasty and every face wore a fierce scowl.

Dylan went racing ahead, desperately trying to find an escape route. He spotted a Viking standing guard behind a tank that had its engine running. If only he could distract the

guard for a few seconds.

'Hey! Your shoelaces are undone!' he cried.

The Viking looked at Dylan in utter bewilderment. 'What are shoelaces?' he asked.

'Oh, never mind,' shouted Dylan impatiently and gave the Viking an almighty kick on his left shin.

'Aaargh! That hurt! Aaargh! And so did that!' cried the Viking as Dylan kicked his right shin. The Viking quickly discovered that trying to lift both legs off the ground at the same time was Not A Good Idea and went crashing to the ground. The runaways piled into the tank.

'I'll drive,' the doctor yelled at Dylan. 'You give me directions!'

The tank gave an almighty lurch and, suddenly, they were moving at high speed, scattering Vikings in every direction as the tank crashed about.

'Left!' ordered Dylan. 'I said left, not right. Go right now. Right. Right! RIGHT!! No! Left!

Forwards, not backwards! CAN'T YOU DRIVE PROPERLY?'

'I never passed my driving test,' admitted the doctor. 'I ran over the examiner and he didn't like me after that.'

'LEFT!' screamed Dylan as the tank nearly drove through a massive tent.

It carried on like a giant tin elephant trying to eat its own tail. It went round in circles. It went round in triangles. It went round in squares. Finally, it went round in a Very Bad Mood as Dylan got fed up with the doctor's impossible driving.

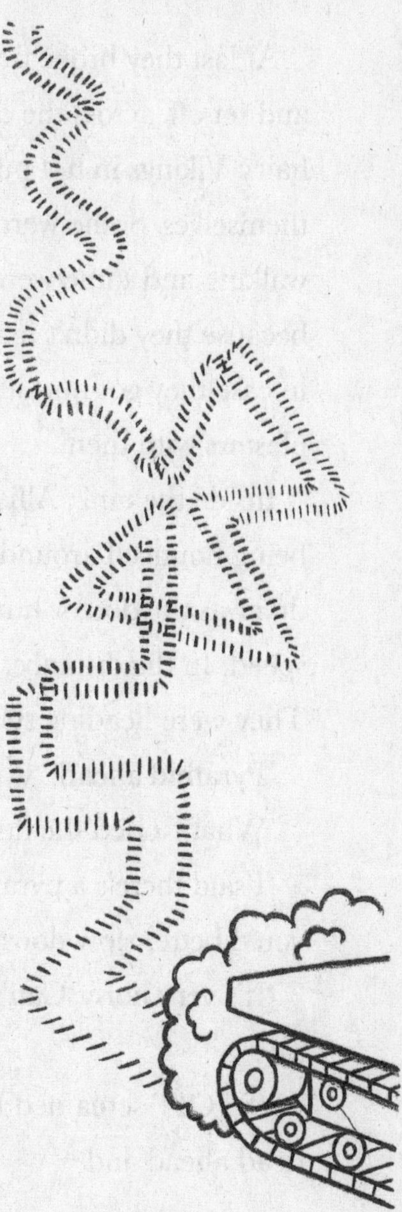

At last they broke free of the Viking camp and set off across the desert, with a thousand hairy Vikings in hot pursuit. Some were in tanks themselves. Some were running. Some were walking and some were dawdling at the back, because they didn't really want to get involved in case they got hurt and they didn't have any plasters with them.

Inside the tank, Alfie, Rosie and Bandit were being bounced around like tennis balls in a spin dryer as the doctor hurtled across the sand at top speed. In the distance, Dylan spotted a pyramid. They were heading straight for it, closing fast.

'Pyramid ahead!' warned Dylan.

'What?' cried the doctor.

'I said there's a pyramid ahead. It's pretty close, you'd better slow down.'

'It's very noisy. Can't hear you. What did you say?'

'STOP!' screamed Dylan. 'There's a pyramid dead ahead and –'

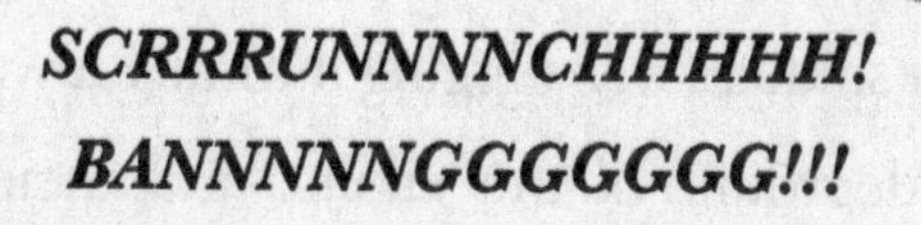
SCRRRUNNNNCHHHHH!
BANNNNNGGGGGGG!!!

4¼ Meanwhile . . .

Several metres beneath the desert a lot of digging was going on. A whole regiment of Roman soldiers was digging a tunnel towards the battleground of the Vikings and ancient Egyptians. It was very hot in the tunnel and rather smelly. Several hundred sweaty Roman soldiers all

jumbled together make for a lot of BO.

Julius Caesar mopped his brow and looked at his map.

'Another few miles to go and then we shall be there. We'll come to the surface, leap out, seize the Doombuster and vanish into our tunnel again. Won't they be surprised? Ha ha ha ha ha ha!'

And at the same time, thousands of miles away, the *Titanic* peacefully steamed across the ocean.

5 Bandit Shows the Way. Pity it's the Wrong One

There was a dreadful noise as the tank hit the bottom of the pyramid at full speed. The exhaust coughed, belched and burped up a stinking cloud of black smoke as the caterpillar tracks clawed furiously at sand and stone. For a long, wobbly moment the tank was held there, rammed against the base of the pyramid. And then it began to climb, grinding its way up the side at a perilous angle.

Inside, the contents were trying to sort themselves out. Alfie had ended up piled on top of Dylan. Rosie had one leg stuck under Dylan's armpit and the other waving loosely in the air like some strange new plant. Alfie had Bandit draped over his head like a ginger wig. A wig with

a tail. Only Doctor Starkly-Bonkers was still in his seat.

Halfway up the pyramid the tank ground to a halt. It gave one more black burp and decided enough was enough. Besides, it didn't like heights.

The children clambered out, followed by the doctor. Gazing out across the desert they could see a fast-approaching swarm of angry Vikings.

Then, from round the sides of the pyramid, another army appeared. Ancient Egyptians, many of them mounted on dinosaurs, went hurtling towards the enemy.

'Go on!' cried Alfie. 'Go get 'em! Hooray! We're saved!'

'Not quite, I'm afraid,' the doctor pointed out. 'They're also after us.'

It was true. Ancient Egyptian soldiers were starting to clamber up the sides of the pyramid towards them.

Rosie hastily searched for an escape route. 'It looks like there's some kind of entrance higher up. Maybe we can get inside.'

'Good idea,' agreed the doctor. 'Come on.'

'It won't work,' muttered Dylan.

'Got a better idea?' asked Rosie, as an ancient Egyptian spear whizzed past, almost taking off Dylan's ear before clunking harmlessly against the stonework.

'Let's go!' he shouted, hurrying ahead.

They scrambled up to the hole that Rosie had seen. The doctor said it was probably a ventilation shaft and would lead down into the pyramid. They hurried inside. It was dark, hot and smelly. The shaft sloped down at a steep angle and it was hard work to move along it. Behind them they heard the shouts of the pursuing soldiers.

'Now they're in front of us and behind us,' said Dylan gloomily. 'We're trapped.'

'Maybe not. There are more passageways off this one.' The doctor was peering into the darkness of yet another shaft. 'Let's try to lose them all by going down here.'

The new passage didn't go down as steeply as the first and after a few bends they came to a small chamber lit by a single flaming brand. On the far side were two tall statues.

'That's Anubis,' said Dylan, pointing at a man with the head of a jackal. 'He was the God of the Dead.'

'And that's Bast, the Goddess of Protection,' added Rosie, looking at the one with the head of a cat. Bandit trotted across to Bast, brushing up against her feet and purring happily.

'The ancient Egyptians loved cats,' Rosie went on. 'If you hurt a cat you could be put to death.' Bandit looked back at Rosie. He almost seemed to be smiling. He certainly looked pretty smug, but then cats often do.

Alfie plucked at Rosie's hem. 'I'm hungry,' he began.

'Don't you ever stop eating?' Rosie groaned.

'If I don't eat I shall never grow at all. I shall just get smaller and smaller and smaller until you'll need a magnifying glass to see me. So there.'

'I don't think that's very likely to happen,' Rosie told him. 'You'll just have to wait.'

'Isn't there a shop in here?' Alfie moaned.

'No, they didn't have shops in ancient Egyptian pyramids.'

'Why not? There should be a sweet shop and an ice-cream place and a burger bar and chips and everything.' Alfie waved his arms about to show just how big everything was.

Rosie was stumped. Why didn't they have shops? When they did the ancient Egyptians at school the teachers hadn't taught them things like that. She brushed the sweat from her forehead. An ice-cream parlour would be very welcome.

She turned to her little brother.

'Alfie, please be quiet so that we can think of a plan.'

'I've got a plan already,' Alfie declared. 'We get some food.'

'Alfie!' chorused the twins. 'Zip it!'

The doctor sat down against a wall. 'I think we are safe for the time being, but we can't stay here forever. Now then, we know from what the Vikings told us that the ancient Egyptians have got the –' He paused. 'I'm not even going to try to say Doombuster because I always get it wrong.'

'You just said it,' laughed Dylan and Rosie.

'I did? Did I? I said Bootbutter? I mean Who-nutter? Poocluster? See – that's what happens.' The doctor sighed heavily. 'Anyhow, we may well find the you-know-what right here in this pyramid. You saw how quickly the army came out to defend this place from the Vikings. I think that's a good sign that the weapon is here. All we have to do is find it.'

'Without getting caught,' Dylan added.

'Yes,' agreed the doctor.

'And then get it back to the invisible spaceship,' Dylan went on. 'Which will be very difficult to find again because WE CAN'T SEE IT!'

'Yes,' the doctor nodded.

'Without getting caught again,' Dylan finished.

'You're not being very helpful,' the doctor complained. 'We're in enough trouble without you being so awkward.'

'Where do you think we should start looking?' asked Rosie, trying to be useful.

'Good question,' beamed the doctor, brightening up. 'My feeling is that the ancient Egyptians have hidden it somewhere, and the best place to do that would be to put it in a coffin with a mummy.'

Alfie pulled a face. 'Yuck!'

'Maybe, but yucky places are good for hiding things,' the doctor said wisely.

'It's bound to be heavily guarded,' Dylan put

in. 'And if they see us in these Viking clothes we'll be mincemeat. If we take them off we'll be cooler too. It's like an oven in here.'

The doctor raised his eyebrows. 'Now that, young Dylan, is definitely a good idea.'

As they got rid of their Viking garb they tried to decide what to do next. They couldn't go back the way they'd come in case they ran into the soldiers. On the other hand, they couldn't go forward either because there *was* no way forward. They tried as hard as they could, but there didn't seem to be any way out of their problem.

Rosie was sitting next to the doctor, leaning back against the wall. He was studying her pyjamas.

'They're very unusual,' he said. 'The pictures are particularly interesting. I don't know if you have noticed, but they all seem to have something to do with Spice and Tame, Twice in Spain, Face and Spine, Space and Time!'

'I didn't know that,' admitted Rosie.

'Mmm. And I've never seen wriggly writing on pyjamas either,' the doctor went on.

'Wriggly writing? Where?'

'Look, just below your knee,' the doctor pointed.

Rosie and Dylan both stared at her knee. Sure enough, a little snake of letters was slithering around the pictures, making its way down towards her ankle.

THE DOOR OF THE GODS

That was all it said. The Door of the Gods. Even as they watched the word snake, it slowly faded and vanished.

Dylan drew in his breath sharply. 'Those pyjamas are just totally weird,' he declared, backing away. 'They give me the creeps.'

The doctor was frowning and repeating the words to himself over and over again in his usual mixed-up manner. 'Hmm. The Jaw of the Gobs. The Paws of the Dog. The Law of the Puds. What does it all mean?'

Dylan was studying the two statues. Finally, he went over and examined them more carefully. He traced lines with his fingers up the wall while the others watched, puzzled. Then he started pressing the wall in different places. When that got him nowhere he began stamping on the floor, leaping from one stone slab to another, like a small, annoyed kangaroo.

'What are you doing?' asked Rosie.

'Finding a way out,' muttered Dylan, hopping on to another slab.

'You're mad,' Rosie told him.

'And you're –'

SKRREEEEEEEEEKKKKKKK!

With an awful scraping and tearing the two tall statues began to move. Slowly, they shifted away from each other, one to the right and one to the left. Hardly had they stopped when the section of wall between them slowly slid up into the ceiling.

SHWOOOOOOFFFFFF!!

Everyone gawped at the magical doorway.

Beyond lay another room. They gathered at the opening and peered in. The new chamber was much bigger than the one they had been in, and finer. Flaming brands lit the walls. These were painted with beautiful images of ancient Egyptian people going about their everyday work. The floor was made up of coloured stone slabs, all squares and triangles, cleverly fitted together in a locking pattern.

'It's gorgeous.' Rosie's face was full of wonder.

'We must be careful,' warned the doctor. 'I have heard of rooms like this in the pyramids. They are designed to look lovely, but in fact they are deadly traps. We must take care where we walk. I suggest we don't walk on any lines.'

'Suppose it's not the lines that are unsafe?' asked Rosie. 'Maybe it's the spaces between the lines, or the squares, or the triangles.'

Dylan looked at her in despair. 'OK, so if we don't tread on lines or spaces or squares or triangles, that only leaves us the walls and ceiling. Tell you what, Rosie, you go across the ceiling and we'll go round the walls. Or maybe you've got a hot-air balloon in your pocket and we can sail across in that.'

'Oh, very ha ha. You're just being stupid,'

Rosie sniffed. 'I was only saying we don't know which bit is unsafe.'

'We don't even know if *any* of it is unsafe,' Dylan said. 'But we have to get across the room.'

'I'm hungry,' added Alfie predictably.

'Miaow,' Bandit put in for good measure.

Doctor Starkly-Bonkers was tired of their bickering. 'Right,' he declared. 'This is what we are going to do. We must only bare on the beds, I mean head on the bears, ted on the stairs, tread on the squares!'

The doctor edged into the room, closely followed by the others. They began to cross the floor on tiptoe, hearts in mouths and holding their collective breath.

Bandit, being a cat, had a mind of his own and went marching off in a quite different direction. He didn't give two hoots about keeping to squares or tiddling about on tippy-toes like some frilly ballet dancer. Squares and triangles were all the same to him. Alfie went after him.

There was a sudden rumble, quickly followed by a crunching bang and a startled squeak from Alfie as a stone slab in the floor opened up and swallowed both Bandit and Alfie.

SHOOODDOOOFFF! They were gone and before Rosie or Dylan could do anything, the slab slid back into place. ***KRRRRUNNKKK!***

The twins scrabbled madly at the slab, but

it was no good. Rosie was aghast and looked helplessly at the doctor. 'We've lost Alfie and Bandit! What are we going to do?'

The doctor had no idea. He hurried across to the stone, but before he was halfway there the ground opened up beneath his feet and Doctor Starkly-Bonkers vanished too.

SHURRRRUPPPPP! KRRRRUNNNNKKK!

Dylan and Rosie stared at the empty space where the doctor had been a moment earlier. The chamber filled with a deadly silence. They stared all around at the sea of squares and triangles, not knowing where to tread next.

Rosie's face was white. 'We've lost Alfie,' she whispered. 'What are we going to tell Mum and Dad?' As she stared hopelessly at Dylan a tear ran down her cheek.

5¼ Meanwhile . . .

Thousands of miles away the *Titanic* was slicing through the waves towards its date with destiny.

And deep beneath the desert Julius Caesar was making very good progress in his tunnel, although he had plugged his nostrils with bits of cloth. The sweaty stink from the hundreds of digging soldiers really was getting to him. He had almost reached his destination and now he rubbed his hands together with glee.

'Soon! It will be very soon! I shall have the Doombuster in my hands and then I shall be able to destroy all my enemies in one go and I shall RULE THE WORLD! This will be my master stroke! Ha ha ha ha ha ha ha ha ha ha ha!'

6 What a Load of Rubbish

'*HEEEEEEEEEEEEEEEEEEEELP!!!*'

FLUMMMMPPPP!!

Hardly had Alfie landed with a thud than a wild ginger hairpiece landed on his head, gave a dismayed screech and leapt off, straight into an old bucket. Bandit peered out angrily. A moment after that an even bigger lump of rubbish came hurtling down from above, all arms and legs, and crash-landed on what was actually a huge ancient Egyptian rubbish heap.

'***AAAAAAAAARGH – URRRKKKKK – SSPLURRRPP!!***'

It was the doctor. He lay there on his back, winded and slightly stunned. Alfie sat up and held his nose. 'This place stinks!' he observed.

This was hardly surprising. The place was,

after all, a rubbish tip. It was made of old banana skins, rotting wood, strips of cloth, smelly, broken sandals, fish bones, chicken carcasses, half-chewed food, smashed plates, slime, creepy-crawlies and several hundred rats.

'We must have fallen right through the Earth,' Alfie declared proudly.

The doctor groaned, shifted uneasily and managed to raise himself on one elbow. He found himself peering straight into an eyeless skull. He shuddered and then realized the skull was attached to a whole skeleton, propped against the wall of the rubbish tip. One bony arm was stretched out, as if it was pointing at something.

'That was an amazing slide,' Alfie said, before asking where the others were.

'I'm afraid we've got separated,' the doctor answered, picking a fish head out of his hair and tossing it to one side.

'Oh.' Alfie considered this for a few seconds. 'Have you got anything to eat? I'm hungry.'

The doctor was amazed by Alfie's one-track mind. 'We are missing your brother and sister,' he said. 'We should try to find them.'

'OK,' said Alfie. 'But some food would be good.'

The doctor studied the skeleton. He was trying to see if it really was pointing at something.

'I think that might be the way out,' he said to Alfie. 'Over there, where the skeleton is pointing.'

'Is that skeleton real?' Alfie asked.

'Yes.'

'So was it a real person before it became a skeleton?'

'Yes.'

'Oh.' Alfie thought. 'So did that person die in here?'

'Probably.'

'I bet he died of starvation,' suggested Alfie.

'I expect so,' nodded the doctor.

'I think we should get out before we die of starvation,' Alfie said.

'Good idea,' said the doctor, pleased that Alfie at last agreed with him.

They crawled across the rubbish pile to where the skeleton was pointing, scattering rats in all directions. Sure enough, they found a metal grid stuck in the wall.

Doctor Starkly-Bonkers looked at it for a long time and then delivered his opinion.

'The ancient Egyptians must have to clear out this rubbish tip from time to time. This will be where they get in and out. There are grooves on both sides of the frame and a gap above. My guess is that the grid slides into the gap.'

The doctor tried lifting the grid himself, but it wouldn't budge. Alfie and Bandit came over to add their muscle power. Bandit didn't exactly add his, but he did watch the other two with great interest. There was a lot of panting and grunting and all of a sudden the grid broke free and shot straight up into the gap.

The doctor looked back at the pointing skeleton and wondered how long it had been there, waiting to show them the way out. 'Sorry, old chum,' he murmured quietly. 'But thanks for your help.' He turned away to join Alfie and Bandit as they clambered out.

They were in a long passageway, faintly lit by burning brands. The ceiling above them was curved, so it was like being in a tunnel. It stretched away in both directions.

'Well, Alfie,' said the doctor. 'We can either go right or left. Which way do you think would be best?' he asked, thinking that the right looked quite promising.

'Left,' said Alfie.

The doctor's brow screwed itself up into an annoyed frown. He was convinced that going to the right would be better. The solution suddenly came to him and he reached into a pocket. 'Let's toss a coin.'

'OK,' Alfie said happily. 'Tails.'

'Heads,' chose the doctor and he spun the coin into the air. It fell to the ground. Tails. The doctor stooped and picked up the coin. 'Heads it is,' he told Alfie. ' We go right. Sorry.'

'Are you sure?' asked Alfie.

The doctor lifted his nose a fraction and sniffed the air to the right. 'I think I smell food that way,' he suggested.

Alfie sniffed too. 'I can't smell anything,' he said bluntly.

'Well, I can. How about we go right and take a look?' the doctor urged. 'Come on, we can't hang around here all day.'

He began to march down the passage. Alfie and Bandit soon fell in beside him.

The doctor became deep in thought. First of all he was wondering if the Doombuster was likely to be hidden anywhere near where they were.

Then his thoughts drifted back to the rubbish tip. He was still finding bits of old banana skin in his pockets and down his shirt. Smelly as the dump had been, it was a good thing it was there. At least they'd had a soft landing. And he also began to wonder, if the banana skin itself was ancient, which it certainly was, would that make it an *ancient* ancient Egyptian banana skin?

The doctor was just playing with the idea that it might even be an ancient Egyptian's ancient ancient Egyptian banana skin when he turned a corner and there, at the end of the passage, was a real patrol of real ancient Egyptian guards, along with a couple of velociraptors.

'Oh dear,' he murmured. The velociraptors, which were like small, yappy tyrannosauruses, immediately spotted the doctor and Alfie. They howled and barked with fury, tore the leads out of the hands of their handlers, and came tearing after the adventurers.

'Run for it!' yelled the doctor.

'What are they?' squealed Alfie as he tried to keep up.

'They're bellycopters, I mean colossitractors, velociraptors!' the doctor cried. 'And they eat FLESH!'

Bandit went pounding ahead. He wasn't

bothered about stopping to say 'Hello, how are you?' to a couple of velociraptors who had very big mouths and lots of teeth. They reached the grate in the wall that marked the rubbish heap.

'I told you we should have turned left!' panted Alfie. 'And I'm getting a stitch. I can't run any more.' He stopped, bent double in pain.

The doctor slammed on his brakes, scooped Alfie up from the ground, tucked him under his arm and started off again. The velociraptors were closing fast, slobbering and slavering, mouths flecked with foam and their eyes bright with hunger. *SNAP! SNAPPITY-SNAP!*

The ancient Egyptian guards came hurrying along behind them, waving spears and shouting, 'Stop! In the name of the Pharaoh Tutankummin.'

But of course the doctor didn't stop, no matter what the pharaoh's name was. He kept running and soon they rounded a corner and there, slap bang in front of them, was a Tyrannosaurus rex.

Plus, there were five triceratopses, a brontosaurus, eight stegosauruses – or was it nine? And a large flock of pteranodons. And a woolly mammoth. Not to mention two stegosauruses pulling a refuse cart.

The doctor almost ran straight into them. He froze on the spot instead. This was way beyond him. What was he to do now? They had velociraptors and guards waiting behind and a zoo-sized collection of bone-crunching dinosaurs

in front. Not to mention the woolly mammoth.

It was a good thing Bandit was there. As the tyrannosaurus stepped forward with open jaws, showing off some very, *very* sharp teeth and a rather unpleasant tongue, Bandit stepped up too. He advanced until he was almost nose to toe with the tyrannosaurus, looked straight up into the monster's glittering yellow eyes, and hissed – '***SSSSSSSSSSSSSSSSSSSSSSSS!***'

The tyrannosaurus lifted his head sharply. Bandit hissed and spat and the giant lizard took a step back, then another and another. All the dinosaurs slowly backed off, turning away and wandering off, trying to look as if they weren't scared, it was just that they'd remembered they'd left the kettle on at home.

Bandit turned his attention to the velociraptors, hissing at them. They did exactly the same thing, except they were even more scared and went scooting back to their owners, the guards, and hid behind them. The ginger warrior fluffed out his tail and began to wash it.

Alfie ran to the cat. 'You are so brave and brilliant!' he cried, almost hugging the moggy to death.

But the four guards were certainly not scared of a cat. They marched forward, spears at the ready, surrounding the doctor, Alfie and Bandit. Their leader, Shutshed, growled his orders.

'Come with us,' he snarled, and they were marched away.

7 A Bit of a Pile-up

Meanwhile, far above the dinosaurs, the rubbish heap and the never-ending tunnels, Dylan was hugging Rosie because she was so upset. Dylan was careful not to hug her for *too* long. After all, he didn't want her to think that he cared for her *that* much. (Although of course he did. He simply didn't want her to know it.)

'I hate your cosmic pyjamas,' he said, 'but don't worry. I'm going to get us out of here.'

'How? Anything we tread on might be a trap,' Rosie sniffed, gazing forlornly round the chamber.

'I think the green triangles are OK. The doctor was treading on the green triangles before anything happened. Follow me. I'll go ahead and test each slab with one foot, all right?'

'Do you think we'll ever find Alfie?' Rosie asked.

Dylan gave an emphatic nod. 'Of course we will. All we have to do is find the nearest place for food and that's where he'll be. You know what he's like.' At least that put a pale smile on Rosie's equally pale face.

By this time they were halfway across the room and making good progress. That was when it happened. Maybe the triangle wasn't a proper triangle. Maybe it was the wrong kind of green. Or maybe Dylan's luck had just run out.

Whatever it was, the slab they were on suddenly gave way.

Dylan just had time to say 'Uh-oh!' and they disappeared straight down a whirling, corkscrewing chute. Down and round they went until suddenly they came flying out through a wall and into a large room filled with dirty washing.

FFLLUMMPPPP!!

They landed on a pile of dirty linen. They sat up, hearts thundering, breathless, and wondering if this was where the doctor, Alfie and Bandit had arrived too. It was quickly clear that it wasn't.

'At least we got out of that horrible room,' Dylan said. 'And we're together.' The thought of being on his own put a chill in his heart.

Rosie was examining some of the dirty linen and pulling a disgusted face.

'This place must be a laundry,' Rosie mused, holding up something that looked very like a pair of ancient Egyptian underpants. 'Urggh!'

'So what do we do now?' asked Dylan, sitting on a rather wobbly pile of linen that came in all shapes and sizes.

'We have to find Alfie and Bandit and the doctor – not to mention the Doombuster,' Rosie sighed. 'But I don't even know where to start. They could be anywhere. And how are we going to search for *them* in a pyramid that's crawling with ancient Egyptians who are looking for *us*?'

Gloom descended. Neither of them could think of anything except the possibility of getting caught. There was a long spell of silence and then Rosie said, very quietly, 'We can't go home without them.'

'Huh! We can't get home at all, can we?' Dylan said gruffly. 'We don't even know how we got here, apart from it being your stupid jim-jams. Honestly, when you put on a pair of pyjamas, you're supposed to go to bed, not to a completely different planet!'

Rosie looked at her pyjamas with disgust. And

there, crawling up her right arm, was a message.

WEAR A SKIRT

Rosie wondered if she should bother to tell Dylan. She was tired and fed up and the last time the pyjamas had sent them a message they had ended up in a chamber full of traps and got separated from Alfie, Bandit and the doctor. She watched the message until it reached her shoulder and then faded away.

Rosie sat in thought, idly pulling at the bits of laundry around her. What difference would a skirt make? Why a skirt? Why not trousers? Or a dress? Why should it be a skirt? Then she began to recall some of the paintings in the beautiful but deadly chamber. There were pictures of ancient Egyptians – soldiers, kings, priests, workers, all sorts. And they all wore white skirts.

Of course! The ancient Egyptians who had chased them up the pyramid wore skirts. It was so obvious. Rosie jumped to her feet and began pulling at the linen that lay about her.

'I thought these were sheets,' she cried.

'They are.'

'No, they're skirts – ancient Egyptian skirts. We can wear these as a disguise!'

'I'm *not* wearing a crummy skirt,' Dylan spluttered.

'Dylan, it's what all the men wore in ancient Egyptian times.'

'So? I'd rather walk about in my pants than wear a skirt.'

'Fine. You walk around like a jelly-brain and get yourself caught; I'm going to disguise myself.' Rosie began wrapping the skirt round her waist.

'You're still wearing your pyjamas,' Dylan nit-picked.

'And you're still wearing your trousers,' Rosie shot back.

'Didn't say I wasn't going to.'

They carried on in silence, with Rosie trying to wrap the skirt round herself without it falling down. It fell down round her ankles four times. Dylan burst out laughing.

Rosie's answer was to toss a skirt across to her brother. 'Here. You're obviously very clever, so you can show me how to do it.'

Dylan quickly discovered for himself that dressing in an ancient Egyptian skirt when nobody has given you lessons is very difficult. He had the same problem as Rosie.

'This is great,' muttered Dylan. 'I've no idea how they kept their skirts up. They must have nailed them on or something.' He searched the piles of clothing and eventually found some long, thin strips that they could use to tie round them like belts.

'There,' said Rosie, with just a hint of triumph. 'You look fine. Come on.' And she led the way from the laundry room. The Alfie Hunt had begun.

They crept out into a passage and immediately ran into two ancient Egyptian soldiers.

'Leave the talking to me,' hissed Dylan quickly as the soldiers approached. They looked Dylan up and down very suspiciously. One of them had an enormous nose and the other had eyes that looked in two different directions at once.

'What's that you're wearing?' asked Big Nose.

'What do you think I'm wearing?' Dylan demanded. 'A cream bun? Anyhow, what's that you're wearing?'

Big Nose was taken aback and looked at his own perfectly neat skirt. 'What's wrong with it?' he asked.

Dylan laughed. 'It's only like totally out of date!'

Walleye stepped forward. 'What's that stuff underneath your skirt? What's that all about?'

'It's for the cold, you donkey – what did you think it was for? Aren't you cold?' Dylan asked. He was beginning to feel braver and braver.

'Yeah, I'm cold,' agreed Walleye. 'But I've never seen anything like that before.'

'It's the latest fashion,' Dylan said. 'Just come in. Not even the pharaoh has gear like this. Why don't you try some of it out for yourselves? You'll be a lot warmer with this extra stuff on.'

Dylan gave a little twirl to show off and his skirt fell round his ankles. ***SHLUNKK!*** He froze in horror. The soldiers examined the twins with enormous suspicion.

'Are you spies?' asked Walleye.

'Don't be daft,' answered Dylan, reddening, and he tried to laugh it off. 'Ha-ha . . . ha.' He bent down, picked up his skirt and began to tie it round his waist.

Walleye turned to Big Nose. 'I've never seen anyone tie their skirt on like that before. He's a spy if ever I saw one. And so is the other one. I mean, what's that top all about, with all those funny pictures? Spies, both of them.'

Bignose lowered his spear so the point was almost pressing against Dylan's stomach. 'Right, you two. You're under arrest. We're going to take you to the supreme commander. Have you got anything to say?'

'Yes,' said Dylan, turning to Rosie. 'RUN FOR IT!'

And with that they turned tail and legged it down the passage, tearing off their skirts and flinging them behind as they went. Rosie's skirt landed very neatly over Big Nose's head. As he struggled to pull it from his face, he managed to trip Walleye with his spear. Walleye went sprawling in front of Big Nose, who promptly fell on top of him.

The soldiers struggled to their feet, quarrelling over their spears because Big Nose had picked up Walleye's by mistake and Walleye didn't like Big Nose's because he said the handle was all sweaty. Big Nose said he wasn't the least bit sweaty and, in any case, Walleye had bad breath. Finally, they decided it might be an idea to try to catch the spies, and they set off in hot pursuit.

In the meantime, Dylan and Rosie were sprinting away at top speed.

'Keep running!' cried Dylan, glancing behind

and seeing the soldiers catching up. They sped round the corner and almost crashed into a cart full of vegetables being pulled along by a triceratops with an ancient ancient Egyptian farmer sitting astride the beast's fat neck. (He was an ancient ancient Egyptian because he was very old. He had more wrinkles than a tortoise that hadn't been ironed for a month.)

'Get on the cart!' Dylan yelled at his sister. As she clambered on to the back of the wagon Dylan pulled the poor farmer from his perch and took his place.

'Oi! You!' Dylan shouted at the triceratops. 'Get moving!' He poked the lumbering beast

with a stick and, following a gigantic jolt that almost tossed Rosie to the ground, they were off. The cart rumbled forward, with Big Nose, Walleye and the ancient ancient Egyptian farmer steaming after it.

'Stop that cart!'

'Get the spies!'

'Er . . . er . . . someone's stolen my triceratops,' complained the bemused farmer.

The triceratops picked up speed and soon it was doing a lumbering gallop, its huge three-horned head bouncing up and down as it thundered along. Rosie sat on the back of the cart hurling melons, bananas and oranges at the

soldiers. She even managed to score several hits, and soon the soldiers were covered in bits of fruit and lots of pips. They looked very colourful, but squidgy.

Dylan had no idea where they were going, but at least they were escaping from the soldiers, who were now struggling to keep up as they skidded around on banana skins and old melon rind.

Everything would have been fine for the escapers if there hadn't been a fully loaded refuse cart coming in the opposite direction, pulled by two stegosauruses.

'What is this? Some kind of motorway?' shouted Dylan in despair. 'Where are the brakes on this thing?!' But it was already too late.

KRRRASSSHHH! THUDDD! KERRANNNNGGGGG! SSPPPING! '***OW!***'

The three beasts collided. Dylan was catapulted over the triceratops's head and landed on the rubbish wagon. The carts slewed round. A wheel came off Dylan's cart, spilling fruit every which way. Most of that promptly got mashed to bits by the stamping dinosaurs. The shafts on the refuse cart snapped off and it tipped up, dumping a stinking pile (including Dylan) on top of the fruit.

Luckily, Rosie had been thrown to the side and had suffered nothing worse than landing on top of a mashed-up watermelon, leaving her with a wet bottom covered in black pips.

At this point, Big Nose and Walleye, wading through an ever increasing flood of fruit and rubbish, finally caught up with the twins.

Big Nose grinned triumphantly. 'Now the Pharaoh Tutankummin will decide how you die!' he said gleefully.

7¼ Meanwhile . . .

Dig! Dig! Dig! Shovel! Shovel! Shovel! Beneath the desert, squadrons of Roman soldiers dug away at the last remaining section of tunnel. By this time it was almost a thousand miles long. It had gone all the way from Rome, down Italy, under the Mediterranean Sea and beneath Africa. Now, at last, they were about to surface and grab the Doombuster.

Julius Caesar relaxed in his fold-up bed. (He was a bit folded up too because there wasn't much space in the tunnel.) He slowly ate a grape.

'Tomorrow we shall rise up out of the sand and I will become MASTER OF THE UNIVERSE! Ha ha ha ha ha ha ha ha ha ha ha ha ha ha ha ha ha ha ha ha ha!

And thousands of miles away, the *Titanic* sailed quietly on.

8 Bow Down Before the Supreme and Mighty Commander!

'You really do not have to keep poking me,' insisted Dylan.

'Shut up and keep walking,' Walleye growled back at him.

They had left the pyramid. Walleye and Big Nose were marching the two children across the sand towards the pharaoh's palace. It was a thunderingly massive building and it looked about as welcoming as a bath full of crocodiles. Funnily enough there seemed to be a rather large number of crocodiles about the place.

All along the front there were gigantic, identical statues of Pharaoh Tutankummin holding a crocodile under each arm. Not only that, but Rosie and Dylan spotted several palace

guards who appeared to have crocodiles on leads.

'They must be guard crocs,' Dylan whispered to his sister. 'Ow! Stop poking me!'

'No talking,' rasped Walleye.

The prisoners had to climb a hundred and seventy-nine steps simply to reach the palace entrance. Inside, huge pillars supported a ceiling that was so high they could see clouds drifting beneath it.

Flaming torches flickered against the walls. They threw strange shadows across paintings of everyday ancient Egyptian life. There were crocodiles lunching on dinosaurs; flying crocodiles attacking Vikings; two-headed, six-legged crocodiles chasing Vikings; and crocodiles on wheels with tank turrets on their backs, firing at Vikings – that sort of everyday ancient Egyptian life.

'What's with all the crocodiles?' asked Dylan.

Big Nose grunted. 'The mighty Pharaoh Tutankummin likes crocodiles. He is very fond of them.'

Guards were everywhere. Patrols marched past from time to time, criss-crossing the palace. Sentries kept watch at every pillar, every door, every stairway.

They pressed deeper into the palace. Now they came to a great hall. A line of guards stood on duty at the entrance and Big Nose halted in front of them.

'We have two prisoners. We think they are the missing spies.'

The chief guard was Shutshed, the one who had caught Alfie, Bandit and the doctor. Rosie and Dylan, of course, didn't know this.

'Excellent,' Shutshed growled. 'They will be taken before the Supreme and Mighty Commander.'

'Not the pharaoh?' questioned Walleye with surprise.

'The pharaoh is mighty,' Shutshed agreed, 'but not as mighty as Alfenramen. Alfenramen has come to us. He is one of the gods, come down from the sky to be with us here on Earth! We have been blessed. The prisoners will be dealt with by Alfenramen. You may go, and it looks as if you need a good bath and some clean clothes. You stink like pigs and look like them too. I will take charge of the prisoners now.'

Big Nose and Walleye dutifully marched off, but not before Big Nose had a final sneer at them. 'Your days are numbered, spies! Now the gods will decide how you die!'

Shutshed and his guards closed round Dylan and Rosie and they were marched into the depths of the great hall.

'What do you think is going to happen to us?' Rosie asked her brother. Dylan shrugged.

'I just hope it's quick,' he muttered.

'What about Alfie? He's only six,' Rosie went on, her voice close to breaking.

'Sssh!' hissed Shutshed. 'We are coming to the royal chamber. You must not speak. When you reach the stairs to the Supreme Being's throne, you must throw yourself full-length on the floor and beg for mercy. That way you may at least save your lives. You must not look at the Supreme Being or he will turn you into maggots or something worse.'

'Huh. What's worse than maggots?' asked Dylan.

'Rice pudding,' Rosie suggested. 'And Christmas cake.'

Shutshed poked them both with his spear. 'And

you must not speak, either,' he added curtly.

SKRINNNGGG! SKRANNGGG!!
SKREEEEEEEEEEKKKKKKKK!!!

A fanfare of tuneless trumpets and clanking cymbals suddenly filled the air with what sounded like a grand piano crashing into a million saucepans at high speed.

A giant stepped forward. He was MASSIVE. Not only was he as tall as an elephant, but he was built like one too. His head was completely bald and shiny and his ears stuck out. His neck was as thick as an elephant's leg. His body bulged with huge muscles and in his hands he held a very long, very shiny and very sharp executioner's sword.

'That man is holding a very big tin opener,' Dylan whispered to his sister. Rosie didn't laugh. She was too busy having kittens. About thirty-six of them.

'Ssssh!' hissed Shutshed.

The giant swished his mighty sword, glared at

the prisoners, opened his mouth and bellowed. In a very high and squawky voice.

'Prisoners, step forward and throw yourselves upon the mercy of the Supreme Being, Alfenramen, and Pharaoh Tutankummin.'

The squeaky voice sounded so silly coming out of the mouth of a giant that Rosie and Dylan doubled up. They couldn't help themselves.

'Are you laughing at me?' screamed the giant, his eyes bulging like a frog that had swallowed an airbag.

'No,' choked Rosie, through her gritted, giggling teeth. The two prisoners reached the royal steps and lay down upon the ground, faces to the floor. Above them, the giant began squawking to the Supreme Being.

'O, Alfenramen, High Priest and Knower of All Things Knowable and Unknowable and also the Things We're Not So Sure Of, these prisoners were found in the Great Pyramid of your father, Sennapod – He Whose Name Shall Rumble

Down The Ages. They are spies from afar. What is to be done with them?'

A yell interrupted from the top of the royal steps. 'Thwow them to the cwocodiles!'

'Doesn't sound too good so far,' whispered Dylan. 'Shall we run for it?'

'Where to?' asked Rosie.

'Thwow them to the cwocodiles!' repeated the very unpleasant voice. 'Snip snap, cwunch cwunch, it's time for cwocodile lunch! Ha ha ha ha ha ha!'

A different voice interrupted. 'No, wait a minute.'

The new voice was familiar to both the twins. Rosie lifted her head slightly and looked up, hoping that she wouldn't suddenly turn into a maggot or, worse still, a Christmas cake. She didn't, but she did almost choke with surprise.

'Dylan, I have just seen the Supreme Being. Do you know who it is? It's Alfie! He's sitting up there on the throne with Bandit right next to him, wearing a huge robe.'

'Bandit's wearing a robe?' asked Dylan.

'Not the cat, jelly-brain – Alfie.'

'Silence, worms!' screeched the first voice from above. 'I shall have your ears tweaked. I shall have your lips sewn up and your hair pulled out. I shall feed you to the cwocodiles and bears and lions and tigers and . . . and . . . and nibbly things, like ants and earwigs and squiwwels and hamsters –'

'Be silent, Tutankummin!' cried Alfenramen, banging his staff. 'I order you to be quiet. Prisoners, come and stand before me.'

The twins looked up. The Supreme Being – Alfie – sat there, dwarfed by the vast golden robe spread around him. Beneath it all was his plastic Roman armour and on his head, his feathered headdress had been replaced with a pharaoh's crown. In his right hand he held a long, carved, wooden staff and in his left he was still clutching his plastic Utter Death space-gun.

And behind Alfie and Bandit stood Doctor Starkly-Bonkers, giving them little waves and grinning madly.

'Alfie! Doctor! You're OK!' cried Dylan.

Shutshed gave Dylan a hard poke with the sharp end of his spear, sending him sprawling in the dust.

'Show reverence to His Mightiness!' Shutshed growled.

'This is ridiculous,' Dylan hissed angrily, getting to his feet. 'Alfie's six. He's about as mighty as a toilet roll.'

'I will speak with those two,' ordered

Alfenramen, pointing at the twins. 'You may come and stand here.'

'Aha! Now we shall see something nasty,' squawked Tutankummin triumphantly. 'Maybe we can bwing the cwocodiles in here and watch them take a snack?'

The twins ignored the mad pharaoh and went to Alfie's throne. 'What's it all about, Alfie?' Rosie whispered to him.

Little Alfie grinned. 'Isn't it great? They think Bandit's a god. They worship him and call him Bast. They found me with Bandit and they think I'm a god too and I speak for him. I've been put in charge of everything. This whole palace, the whole country, the WHOLE UNIVERSE!'

Dylan groaned. 'The world's gone mad,' he said gloomily, while Rosie beamed with happiness.

'I'm *so* pleased we found you,' she murmured, hugging her little brother.

The doctor spoke for the first time. 'After we fell through the floor, we ended up on a rubbish tip.

We escaped, but got caught. We thought we were in BIG trouble, but we were saved by Bandit. The ancient Egyptians worship a cat god called Bast, and they've decided that Bandit *is* Bast. He's saved our lives – and now yours too. I must say it's very good to see you.'

'I can do anything I want!' Alfie chipped in. 'I had five bowls of rice pudding for breakfast this morning!'

Rosie groaned. 'Alfie! You are disgusting – and so is rice pudding. Besides, you're only six. How can you possibly be a god? It's not fair.'

Alfie glanced towards Tutankummin. 'I don't like him. He's not a god. He's just the pharaoh. He keeps sneering at me and he says nasty things when he thinks nobody else can hear. This is his throne I'm sitting on, but I've been put on it and he doesn't like it. He's jealous.'

'What are you going to do?' Rosie asked.

Alfie shrugged. 'I don't know. I thought you might –'

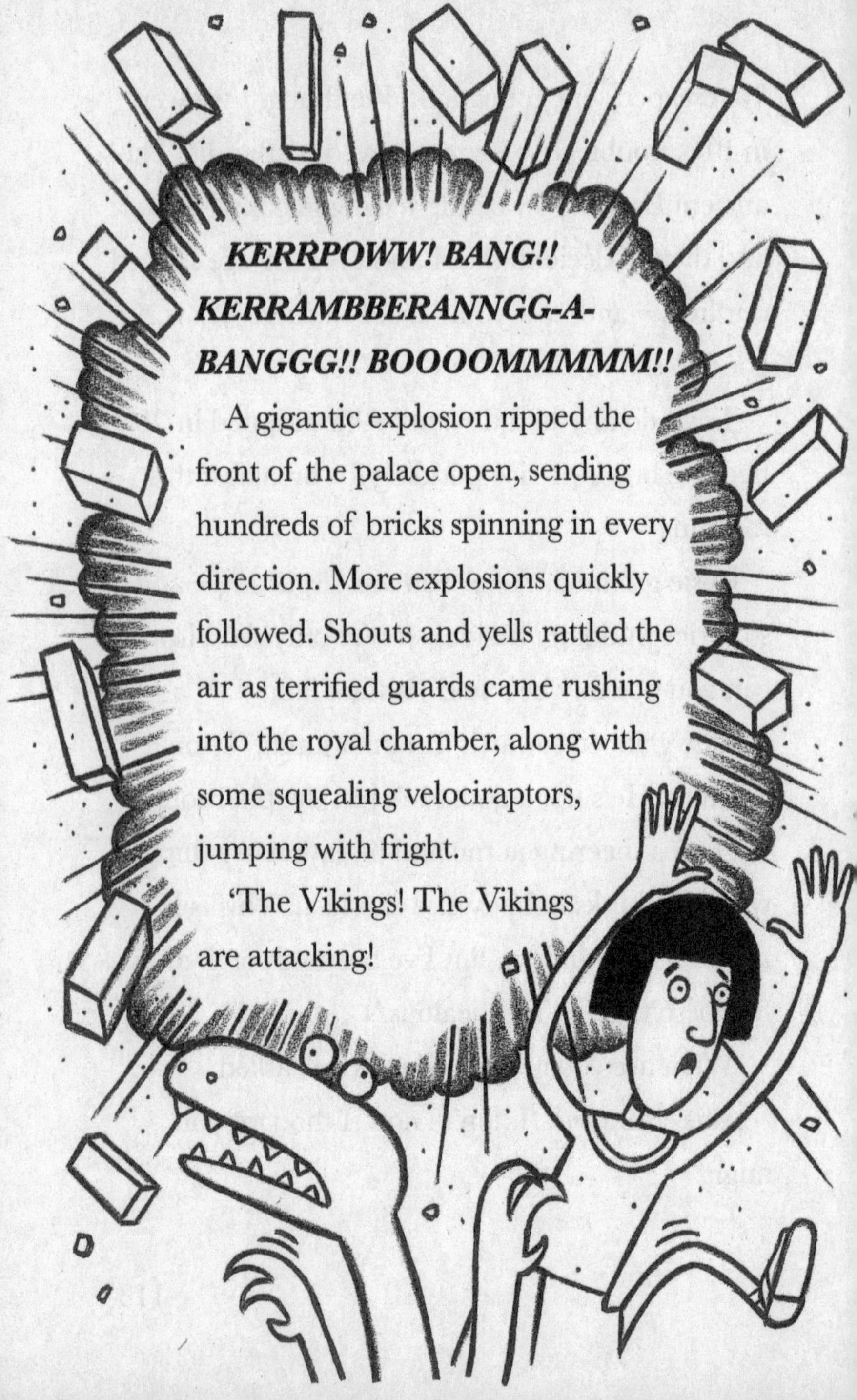

KERRPOWW! BANG!! KERRAMBBERANNGG-A-BANGGG!! BOOOOMMMMM!!

A gigantic explosion ripped the front of the palace open, sending hundreds of bricks spinning in every direction. More explosions quickly followed. Shouts and yells rattled the air as terrified guards came rushing into the royal chamber, along with some squealing velociraptors, jumping with fright.

'The Vikings! The Vikings are attacking!

9 It's Grab-a-Dino Time!

Panic. The guards rushed about, banging into each other, tripping over their spear handles and sprawling in all directions. ***BOOM! BAMM!*** More explosions. Clouds of dust billowed, sending everyone into coughing fits.

Shutshed hurried across to Alfie – or rather Alfenramen – and threw himself at his feet. 'O Highly Mightiness, what shall we do?'

Alfie looked very uncomfortable and gave a startled jolt as another explosion went off nearby. 'Um, can I go home?' he suggested.

Rosie nudged him hard. 'You're a god, Alfie. You must give them orders.'

Alfie's brow wrinkled as he thought hard. At last his face brightened and he got to his feet, scowling at the guards. He was ready to take charge. 'Bring me more rice pudding!' he cried.

The guards were completely mystified. How would rice pudding save them from the Viking attack? ***SPLAMMM!!*** Everyone ducked as another explosion took place. Part of the palace roof caved in, revealing the sky. Viking biplanes circled overhead, dropping bombs.

Although, to be truthful, the planes were not exactly circling. It looked a lot more like they were corkscrewing all over the place. Every so often a plane would fly upside down and a whole Viking would tumble out. ***'AAAAAAARRRRRGGGGGHHHHH!'*** The Vikings were definitely a lot better at sailing longboats than flying biplanes.

The guards began muttering to each other and Shutshed spoke up. 'O Mighty Highly-ness, we are being attacked on all sides and you ask for rice pudding?' The muttering grew, and now Tutankummin stepped forward.

'This new god Alfenwamen is a fool!' he cried. 'We need cwocodiles, not wice pudding. Cwocodiles to eat the Vikings. They will bite off their leggies and armies and cwunch them into small bits!'

'Tutankummin speaks true,' hissed a guard. 'Alfenramen is a useless god.'

Dylan felt a mutiny growing among the guards and began shouting. 'How dare you question

your god! He knows far more than you!'

'Do I?' Alfie looked very confused.

'Sssh,' hissed Dylan. 'Let me finish.' He turned back to the gathering crowd. 'Why does he send for rice pudding? Because Vikings are afraid of rice pudding. Everyone knows that!'

FLABOOMMM! KRUNNGLE-BLUNGGG!

Another explosion and three nearby pillars collapsed, bringing down even more of the roof.

Shutshed frowned. 'I didn't know this. Are you sure? The Vikings are scared of rice pudding?'

Dylan folded his arms and looked down at Shutshed with scorn. 'Be careful,' he advised. He swung one arm wide to point at Bandit. 'This is Bast, your god. He knows everything and has told his servant Alfenramen.'

Bandit looked at Dylan and Shutshed for a moment, lifted one back leg and began to clean his bottom. Tutankummin was not in the least bit impressed.

'Bast? Pah! He is just a ginger moggy. Vikings

afwaid of wice pudding? It's widiculous!'

The guards muttered even more and pressed forward again. Dylan was fighting a losing battle. Tutankummin pressed his advantage.

'You must listen to me. Don't listen to these childwen! I am your phawoh! We must fight the Vikings with cwocodiles! We will thwow cwocodiles at them. We will dwop cwocodiles on them from the top of the pywamid and squash them!'

'Yes, that's the way to beat the Vikings!' roared the crowd, and they banged their spears in support of the young pharaoh.

Dylan tried desperately to think of something, but nothing came into his head. Rosie suddenly grabbed his arm.

'Look! Look at my pyjama sleeve!' Winding their way through all the little pictures on Rosie's left sleeve were three words. They wiggled and wriggled along as they made their way round the hem of her top.

RELEASE THE DINOSAURS!

That's what they said.

'It's incredible,' murmured Dylan. 'Like magic. Look, now they're disappearing.' The words vanished as mysteriously as they had appeared. Rosie bent over Alfie and whispered in his ear.

Alfie got to his feet. He banged his staff on the ground, pointed his plastic space-gun at Shutshed and barked his order. 'Release the dinosaurs!'

Shutshed jerked upright. 'O Highly Mighty Brightiness !' he cried. 'A truly wonderful plan. Dinosaurs are much more powerful than crocodiles. They will mash the Vikings and squash them to a squidge. They will do battle with the dreaded Vikings and we shall be saved. Release the dinosaurs!'

Shutshed spurred on the guards and they all rushed off to save the kingdom. That just left Tutankummin, who was looking as angry and peeved as a teenager could be. The pharaoh hissed at Alfie.

'You're nothing but a little boy!'

'And you're nothing,' Rosie said evenly, coming to the rescue. 'Why don't you go and play with your crocodiles?'

Tutankummin slunk away and as soon as he had gone, Dylan took over. He grabbed Bandit and yanked Alfie from his throne. 'Come on. Let's get out of here.'

BE-DANNGG BE-DOOOMM!!!

'*Quickly*,' coughed Dylan. 'This palace is crumbling round our ears.'

Doctor Starkly-Bonkers made for the throne where Alfie and Bandit had been sitting.

'Just a moment. I must look under here. I have a funny feeling that –' The doctor broke off and stared beneath the seat of the throne. 'At last,' he breathed. He bent over the seat, reached inside and pulled out a long, silver, blue and red sausage.

'Behold! I have the Broomshutter, I mean the Zoomnutter, the Spooncustard, Moonduster,

Doombuster! We have it back! Now we must get to the spaceship as prickly as crossible!'

With Dylan leading they made their way to the outside. A ghastly sight met their eyes. The Vikings were on the rampage everywhere. Tanks were thundering across the desert, but not necessarily in the right direction. The Vikings were still clanking round in circles, crashing into each other, lifting their huge barrels and firing straight into the air. They brought down several of their own planes.

BOOOM! 'Ow! That hurt, porridge-brain! I'm on your side!'

BOOOM! 'Stop it! You've just shot both my wings off! I can't fly now! Aaaargh!'

At that point the dinosaurs came charging out. Hundreds of pterosaurs took to the air, their vast black wings darkening the sky with their heavy flip-flop-flapping.

They swooped down on the Viking biplanes, beating them to matchwood with their great wings or stabbing them with their terrifying beaks. A squadron of gigantic pteranodons drifted across high above and began bombarding the Viking troops with heavy-duty dino poop. (Which, if you have never seen it, is surprisingly similar to rice pudding.)

While all this chaos was going on, the children, Bandit and the doctor headed for the invisible spaceship, wherever that was. But one band of particularly fierce Vikings had spotted the doctor carrying the world's deadliest weapon. A shout went up and they came roaring after them, brandishing their swords and rattling their beards.

'Hurry!' yelled Dylan, but it was hard work running across sand, especially for Alfie, who had the shortest legs. (Apart from Bandit, of course, but at least he had four of them.) Dylan swung Alfie on to his shoulders and gave him a piggyback.

'We'll never make it to the ship at this speed,' panted Rosie in despair.

By this time they were close to the pyramid where they had been captured, and Dylan had an idea.

'This way!' he cried, plunging through one of the entrances.

BERRANNGGG! SHHLUNNKKKK-CLUNNK-BUDDUNGGG!!

A Viking tank scored a direct hit on the pyramid wall above them and stones came tumbling down all around. They hurried inside.

'What are you doing?' demanded Rosie. 'We need the spaceship.'

'I know, I know. Just follow me! This way – come on!' He plunged down a passageway, deep into the pyramid. By this time they were all breathless, but Dylan forced them on and at last they came to the animal park.

Some of the dinosaurs were still there – a few tyrannosauruses and stegosauruses, the triceratops and brontos. They roared and stood on their back legs. They stamped the ground and huffed and puffed. Once again, Bandit went running forward, hissing and spitting, and within seconds all the dinosaurs had backed off.

'That's amazing!' said Rosie.

'It's just what I was hoping,' Dylan answered with a smile. 'This is what happened to Alfie and the doctor. Alfie's been shouting it into my ear while we were running out there. This is our best chance to escape. Grab a dino.'

'You what?' asked Rosie.

'Quick – everyone – find a dino. We're going on the ride of our lives, back to the ship.'

'You're mad!' cried Rosie.

'No, I'm being chased by thousands of Vikings and ancient Egyptians and goodness knows what else and I don't want to be killed. Get on a dinosaur and let's go!' As he spoke, Dylan was clambering up the back of a tyrannosaurus and hauling Alfie up with him. Think big – that was Dylan's motto.

The doctor plonked himself on a triceratops.

'Be careful with that one,' warned Dylan. 'They don't have any brakes.'

Rosie hastily stuffed Bandit down the front of her pyjamas. 'And no scratching this time,' she warned. 'Or I'll throw you overboard.' She gingerly seated herself on a knobbly ankylosaurus.

Dylan swung his monster round. 'Here we go!' he yelled and, with a kick of his feet, launched the tyro forward. Moments later they burst out of the pyramid and into the desert, scattering the Vikings in all directions.

Bouncing madly up and down behind his big brother, Alfie turned in his seat and pointed his Utter Death space-gun at the Vikings.

'Peeyoww! Peeyoww!' he went, and suddenly shouted in triumph. 'I got one! I got one!'

Sure enough, one of the Vikings had hit the ground, but that might have been because he'd tripped on the shoelaces he didn't have.

And then the pterosaurs came screaming down

at the children, with beaks as sharp as mountain peaks and teeth like chainsaws.

10 Can a Big Mess Save the World?

NEEEEEYOOOWWWWWWWWW!

'That was too close for comfort,' cried Rosie as a diving pterosaur almost took off her head.

'I think we are almost there,' the doctor shouted to the others. 'I'm sure the place pip is around here somewhere. I mean, chase blip, face chip, spaceship.'

'Can't you switch off the invisibility shield?' asked Dylan, ducking like crazy as another pterosaur went shooting past, beak wide open. It came so close, Dylan could even see its tonsils!

'If you remember, the button is on the side of the ship,' the doctor answered.

'That is the most stupid thing I have *ever* heard!' yelled Dylan crossly. 'How are we ever supposed to find – Oww!'

KERTHUDDDD! KLANNGGG!!

There was an almighty bang as Dylan's Tyrannosaurus rex went thundering into something very hard, very heavy and very not there at all.

KERPLONKKK! KRRUNNCH!!

That was the noise of Doctor Starkly-Bonkers and his triceratops colliding with what wasn't there, closely followed by Rosie's ankylosaurus. The whole lot fell over. Dylan sat up and shook

his dazed head. What on earth had happened?

'Aha!' cried the doctor triumphantly. 'I knew the spaceship was here somewhere.' He got to his feet and began wandering round, pressing the sides of the invisible ship. Meanwhile, several pterosaurs went crashing straight into it and flopped to the ground, stunned.

'Hurry up, before these horrible things wake up and decide we'd make a nice picnic,' Dylan urged.

SHWOOOOOOFFF!

With a noise like the arrival of Father Christmas down a chimney, the spaceship suddenly appeared before them. The hatch opened and they all tumbled in. The doctor started the engines and moments later, they whooshed into space. Soon they were whizzing silently through a sea of stars in utter peace.

It was the most wonderful moment. The doctor put the ship on to automatic pilot and they settled down to sort things out.

'Is there anything to eat?' asked Alfie.

'No!' the others chorused and burst out laughing. It was the relief.

'Now I must sort out the mess I have made down there,' the doctor explained. 'We have the thingy thing back, you know, the dum-di-dum –'

'Doombuster?' offered Rosie.

'Exactly. I need to use some of the parts from it to build a Time Separator and Redistributor.'

Dylan nodded. 'I guess that will separate time and redistribute it.'

'Who would have thought it?' Rosie murmured.

'But we have one problem,' the doctor went on. 'To make the Time Separator I also need many parts from the spaceship. We can't use the spaceship while I build the machine. We have to land somewhere.' He peered at everyone from beneath his shaggy eyebrows. Rosie was sure they were growing fast.

'On Earth,' the doctor added, so things were quite clear.

'But –' Alfie began.

'But –' Dylan added.

'But –' Rosie shivered.

'Mia–' began Bandit, distressed.

'I know,' sighed the doctor 'We have only just come from there, but we must go back. Don't worry. We will find somewhere quiet, with a little stinkly cream, I mean tinkly stream and sunny trees and the birds going chirpy chirpy. I am sure all will be fine.'

The scientist looked at everyone and they returned his look. Why didn't they believe him? They watched in disappointed silence as he turned the spaceship round and they headed back to Earth.

The doctor found somewhere quiet, but there was no tinkly stream and no sunny trees and no birds going chirpy chirpy. That was because he had landed on the side of a massive iceberg.

It was dark – very dark. And cold – very, VERY cold. Moonlight twinkled on the waves slapping quietly along the towering sides of the iceberg. The only other sound was the creak and squeak of icy chunks rubbing together.

The doctor at least was happy. 'There – you see? No Vikings, no ancient Egyptians. We have no worries. Let's get to work.' He took Dylan by the arm. 'Come, my boy, you can help me build the machine.'

In the engine room, Dylan and the doctor set to. Soon they were up to their ears in coils of different coloured wires. Bits of spaceship lay all around them. Dylan was constantly having to hold this or that while the doctor wired up tiny components or screwed things together, unscrewed things, dropped things, picked them up, and generally made a BIG MESS. Dylan hoped very much that the BIG MESS would work when it was finished.

'There!' the doctor cried triumphantly. 'Help me carry it through to the others.'

'Is that it?' asked Rosie, staring at the extraordinary confusion of wires and bits of metal. 'It looks like mum's knitting after Bandit has played with it.'

'My dear young lady,' the doctor said tetchily, 'this machine will save the world! All we need now is a pigglety botch.'

'A pigglety botch?' repeated Rosie.

'Yes, you know, a diggerty potch, fiddly snotch, digital watch!'

'Oh!' chorused the others, and they all looked at each other.

Dylan had an ordinary watch. Rosie didn't have one at all. They looked to Alfie.

'I've got one at home,' he said cheerfully.

'Surely one of you has a digital watch?' pleaded the doctor. 'How can we put in the dates for everything without a digital watch?'

He collapsed in his seat, hands clasped to

his head and began muttering to himself. 'We have destroyed the engine of the spaceship to make the Time Separator, so now we can't go ANYWHERE. We are stuck on this iceberg FOREVER and the world will NOT BE SAVED. I have wasted my time.'

Rosie went over and sat next to him. 'Surely you can think of something?' she asked hopefully and with her fingers crossed. But the doctor shook his head. He stopped and frowned.

'There's something moving on your pyjamas.'

Rosie was on instant alert. 'Where?' she demanded. 'Show me, quick!'

'Right there,' said the doctor, pointing at Rosie's knee. It was another message.

FIND THE POCKET

'What pocket?' snapped Rosie. 'These pyjamas don't have a pocket. They've never had a pocket.' She got to her feet. The others crowded round to help her look.

'It might have some food in it,' Alfie suggested happily.

'Turn right round,' ordered the doctor.

'Lift your arms up,' said Dylan.

'Oh, come on,' Rosie grumbled. 'You won't find a pocket in my armpit!'

They soon gave up. There was no pocket. The trickle of words faded away. The message had gone. Gloom descended once more. Alfie tugged at Rosie's sleeve.

'Suppose the pocket is *inside* the pyjamas?' he suggested.

'Don't be ridiculous. Nobody would put a pocket inside a pair of pyjamas,' said Rosie, starting to pat herself all over. 'What on earth would be the – oh! What's this?' She was feeling the back of her leg, just above the knee.

'There's something there. Excuse me a moment.' Rosie disappeared into the spacepod, stuck her arm down her pyjama bottoms and fiddled around until she found the strange little pocket. She screamed and rushed back out to the others.

'I don't believe it! It's a digital watch!' Rosie waved the watch and danced and yelled and hurriedly handed it over to the doctor. 'These pyjamas are driving me MAD!'

'We have no time to lose,' the doctor said. 'Listen carefully. First we connect the watch to the Time Separator and Redistributor with some bits of wire. Then we use the Redistributor to gather up all the ancient Egyptians. We reset the watch to ancient Egyptian times and we send all of them back to their own time, Kerpow! Like that!'

'That's clever,' murmured Dylan. 'And I helped make it,' he added proudly.

'Let's hope it doesn't go wrong, in that case,' muttered Rosie.

Doctor Starkly-Bonkers carried on. 'Then we do the same thing for the dinosaurs and the Vikings and for me.' The doctor beamed, but his smile suddenly vanished.

'But we must hurry because I don't think you have noticed that there is a very, very big ship steaming straight towards us and I am sure it is going to crash into our iceberg, Smish-Smash-Whoopsy!'

'It's the *Titanic*!' screamed Rosie.

10¼ Meanwhile . . .

The desert moved. It heaved. It bibbled and bubbled. It even bobbled a bit and then, suddenly – 'TA RA!' Julius Caesar yelled triumphantly, leaping out of the sand, closely followed by a thousand Roman soldiers, armed to the teeth and yelling like crazy demons who'd been stuck in a tunnel for two years, digging.

'Aha!'

'Raaaaargh!'

'Neeeeehah!'

'Mummy!'

'Now we've got you!'

But Julius Caesar and the thousand Roman soldiers hadn't got anything. The spaceship had gone. The Doombuster had gone. The ancient Egyptians were no longer there and neither were the Vikings. The desert was empty and silent.

Caesar gazed around for a long time and slowly lowered his sword. 'Rats!' he exclaimed. 'We're too late.'

His eyes narrowed. (Roman soldiers always narrowed their eyes when they were thinking.) He narrowed his eyes until they were teeny weeny slits. He narrowed them until he couldn't even see. That's how hard he was thinking. All of a sudden, they sprang wide open and a cunning smile played along his lips. Julius Caesar turned to his men.

'I have had an excellent idea! We are going to dig a tunnel all the way to Britain and when we get there we shall INVADE AND TAKE OVER!'

'Hurrah!' cried all the soldiers. They had to say hurrah or they would have been poked with nasty, pointy swords by their commanders. In fact, they were fed up with digging tunnels.

So the soldiers climbed wearily back down into their stinky, sweaty tunnel. Julius Caesar pointed

his sword and gave his orders.

'That way!' he bellowed. 'Britain, here we come!'

Dig, dig, dig. Shovel, shovel, shovel.

And thousands of miles away, upon the ocean, the mighty *Titanic* . . .

11 BLAAAAAAAHHHHHHHHHHH!

The doctor jabbed a finger towards the mega-gigantic, four-funnelled, gazillion-ton ocean liner that was bearing down on them.

BLAAAAAHHHHHHHHHH!!

'Quick – hand me that bit of wire, Dylan!' ordered the doctor as he made the last few connections. 'There is no time to lose. First we set the watch for the ancient Egyptians and now we press the button like this.'

FFWISSSSSSSSSSSSSSSSSS!

It was as if a giant red hand snaked out from the watch. It went arching out, high above their heads. They watched it come back down to Earth in an ever widening ripple. As it touched the planet, a red glow rose up from the ground. It grew and grew in brightness and then suddenly,

SSSSSSSSSSSSSSSSSSIWFF! It was gone, and so were the ancient Egyptians.

'Quickly now,' said the doctor. 'We reset the watch and say goodbye to the Vikings.'

FFWISSSSSSSSSSSSSSSSSSSSS!

The same thing happened and, somewhere in the world, all the Vikings found themselves returned to their own time. The doctor looked at the children and Bandit.

'And now I must leave you and return to my own time. I thank you for all your help. Without you I could not have rescued the –' The doctor smiled, gathered his thoughts and his tongue very carefully, and said, 'The Doom-bust-er! There! First time. And we would not have been able to put everything back as it should be. And now it's goodbye from Clocktor Sickly Barking, I mean Barkly Plonkers, Farty Starkers, Winky Hooters, Stinkly Stonkers, Oh, you know – ME!'

The great scientist reset the watch. He pressed the button.

FFWISSSSSSSSSSSSSS! SSSSSSSSSSSSIWFF!

The glowing red hand came and went and a moment later, Doctor Starkly-Bonkers was no longer on the iceberg. For a brief second the children looked out into the dark sky, but they could see nothing.

BLAAAAHHHHHH!!

Rosie and Dylan spun round; so did Bandit. The *Titanic* was practically crawling up the iceberg.

'It's our turn,' said Rosie urgently. 'Quick, Dylan, set the watch.'

Dylan was iceberg colour from head to toe,

making him almost invisible.

'The doctor was holding the watch,' he choked. 'And he also had the Time Separator and Redistributor. We're stuck!'

BLAAAAAAHHHHHHHHHH!!

'The spaceship!' cried Rosie. 'We can escape in the spaceship!'

'Do you know how to fly it?' asked Dylan.

'No,' said Rosie. 'Surely you do?'

'Why me? I can't fly it,' snapped Dylan.

'But you're a BOY!' squealed Rosie. 'I thought boys did things like that.'

'And you're a GIRL,' Dylan yelled back. 'And you can't do ANYTHING!'

They both rounded on little Alfie. 'Well?' they chorused. 'Can you fly the spaceship?'

'No,' squeaked poor Alfie.

So that just left Bandit.

All three of them turned to the cat.

'Bandit, can *you* fly a spaceship?'

Bandit rolled over and displayed his fluffy

tum, hoping someone, anyone, would give him a good tickle.

'Not helpful,' muttered Dylan, slumping to the ground. He suddenly began laughing, or was he crying? 'What are we arguing about? Nobody can fly the spaceship because the doctor has taken half the engine with him. It'll never fly again. It's all so crazy I could scream!'

He groaned and looked at his sister. 'You and your pyjamas. I can't believe the mess they've got us into. We're all going to DIE now, and it's all because of those poxy pyjamas of yours.'

BLAAAAAAHHHHHHHHHH!!

The *Titanic* was sending up a huge bow wave of foam ahead of it and the iceberg rocked violently. The three children clutched each other, scared out of their pants, and quite possibly their pyjamas too. Alfie was crying. So was Dylan, but that was because Bandit had leapt on to his head and dug his frightened claws into Dylan's scalp.

'I'm sorry!' sobbed Rosie. 'I love you all!'

'Love you!' echoed Dylan.

'Meeeow meeoow,' went Bandit.

It was Alfie who spotted the little flashing picture on Rosie's cosmic pyjamas.

'Look! It's all lit up! It's a pretty picture of our house!' And he touched it.

KERRANNGG BAM SSWIZZZ JOOOOMMFFF!

The world disappeared – no more iceberg, no more *Titanic*. It was just a swirl of colours, a whirlpool of light and dark. The children felt themselves falling, or was it flying? Anyhow, they were travelling faster than the speed of light until –

CRASSSSHHHHHH!

All four of them landed in an almighty heap on Rosie's bed.

FFUDDD!

The bed legs broke and the next thing the children heard was an angry voice stomping up the stairs.

'What on earth is going on up there!' their father bellowed.

Of course nobody believed them. Rosie and Dylan

didn't even bother to tell their parents what had happened. It was Alfie who tried, but Mum and Dad simply looked at him with a tired expression, the one that says, 'Oh, really? Of course – and pigs might fly.'

'It wasn't pigs,' said Alfie breathlessly. 'It was Vikings. And they bombed us from aeroplanes and the ancient Egyptians had all these dinosaurs and some were riding them and then the pteranodons came and bombed the Vikings and it all went crazy and I rode on a Tyrannosaurus rex!'

Dad was hardly even listening. He was inspecting Rosie's bed. 'Completely broken,' he muttered. 'You'll have to sleep on the floor until I can mend it. How many times have I told you lot *not* to jump on your beds?'

The children shrugged and looked at each other. How many times? Hundreds, that's what. They'd never thought they were supposed to count.

Anyway, Rosie secretly thought that sleeping on the floor would be good fun – as long as she never had to wear those cosmic pyjamas again. She changed out of them as soon as she could and handed them over to her mother.

'I thought you liked them,' said Mum.

'I did when I first saw them, but they kind of take you by surprise,' Rosie explained.

Her mother frowned. 'What do you mean – take you by surprise?'

'They just kind of – you know.'

'No, Rosie, I don't. If I knew I wouldn't ask.'

Rosie wrinkled her nose. 'They're itchy,' she said at last. Mum raised her eyebrows, but took the pyjamas from her.

'I'll see if the charity shop wants them,' sighed Mum. 'Looks like I'll have to wash them first. You've sat in something disgusting.'

'It was only a squashed melon,' said Rosie.

'Why on earth did you sit on *that*?' asked Mum.

'I fell off the cart when Dylan crashed it.'

'Your brother crashed a cart? How did he do that?' Mum was aghast.

Rosie shrugged. 'He was riding a triceratops and couldn't get it to stop and we went round a corner and there were these stegosauruses and –'

Mum held up her hand. 'OK, OK. Stop right there. I've had enough of that from Alfie. Go on now. Leave the pyjamas with me.' Mum chuckled and shook her head. 'I wish I had your imagination.'

Rosie gave a little smile and went back upstairs. In her bedroom she shut the door, leant back against it and let out a long breath. Phew! She would never have to wear those pyjamas again. For a brief moment she wondered what might happen to the next person who wore them, but that thought soon vanished from her head. She had better things to do, like finishing off the game she had been playing on Dylan's PlayStation. (Which he was *still* searching for.)

11¼ Meanwhile . . .

On another planet far away, just like Earth, the ancient Egyptians built pyramids and carried on worshipping lots of gods, including cats. Julius Caesar tried to invade Britain, unsuccessfully – the Romans had to come back over a hundred years later. And even later still, the Vikings sailed halfway round the world and fought and farmed and made a bad reputation for themselves even though some of them were probably quite nice, if a bit hairy. (Not the women, of course. Apart from Erik the Red's wife. She had a BEARD!) Later still, the *Titanic* crashed into an iceberg and sank. Doctor Starkly-Bonkers was only five years old when that happened, but somehow he already knew all about it and wasn't surprised.

As for the cosmic pyjamas, they are no longer with Rosie and may well be in a shop near you, so be careful what you wear.

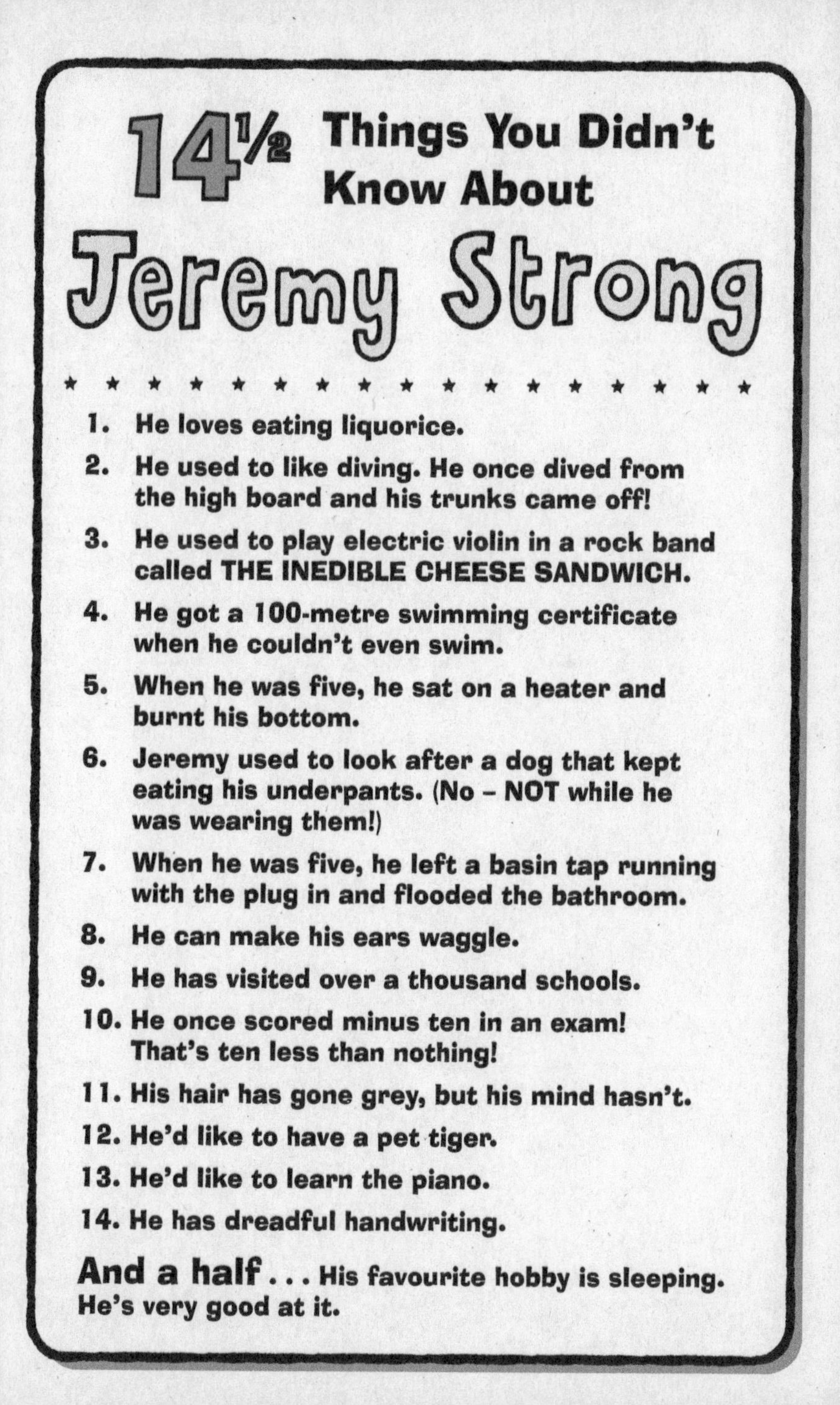

14½ Things You Didn't Know About Jeremy Strong

★ ★ ★ ★ ★ ★ ★ ★ ★ ★ ★ ★ ★ ★ ★ ★ ★

1. He loves eating liquorice.
2. He used to like diving. He once dived from the high board and his trunks came off!
3. He used to play electric violin in a rock band called THE INEDIBLE CHEESE SANDWICH.
4. He got a 100-metre swimming certificate when he couldn't even swim.
5. When he was five, he sat on a heater and burnt his bottom.
6. Jeremy used to look after a dog that kept eating his underpants. (No – NOT while he was wearing them!)
7. When he was five, he left a basin tap running with the plug in and flooded the bathroom.
8. He can make his ears waggle.
9. He has visited over a thousand schools.
10. He once scored minus ten in an exam! That's ten less than nothing!
11. His hair has gone grey, but his mind hasn't.
12. He'd like to have a pet tiger.
13. He'd like to learn the piano.
14. He has dreadful handwriting.

And a half . . . His favourite hobby is sleeping. He's very good at it.

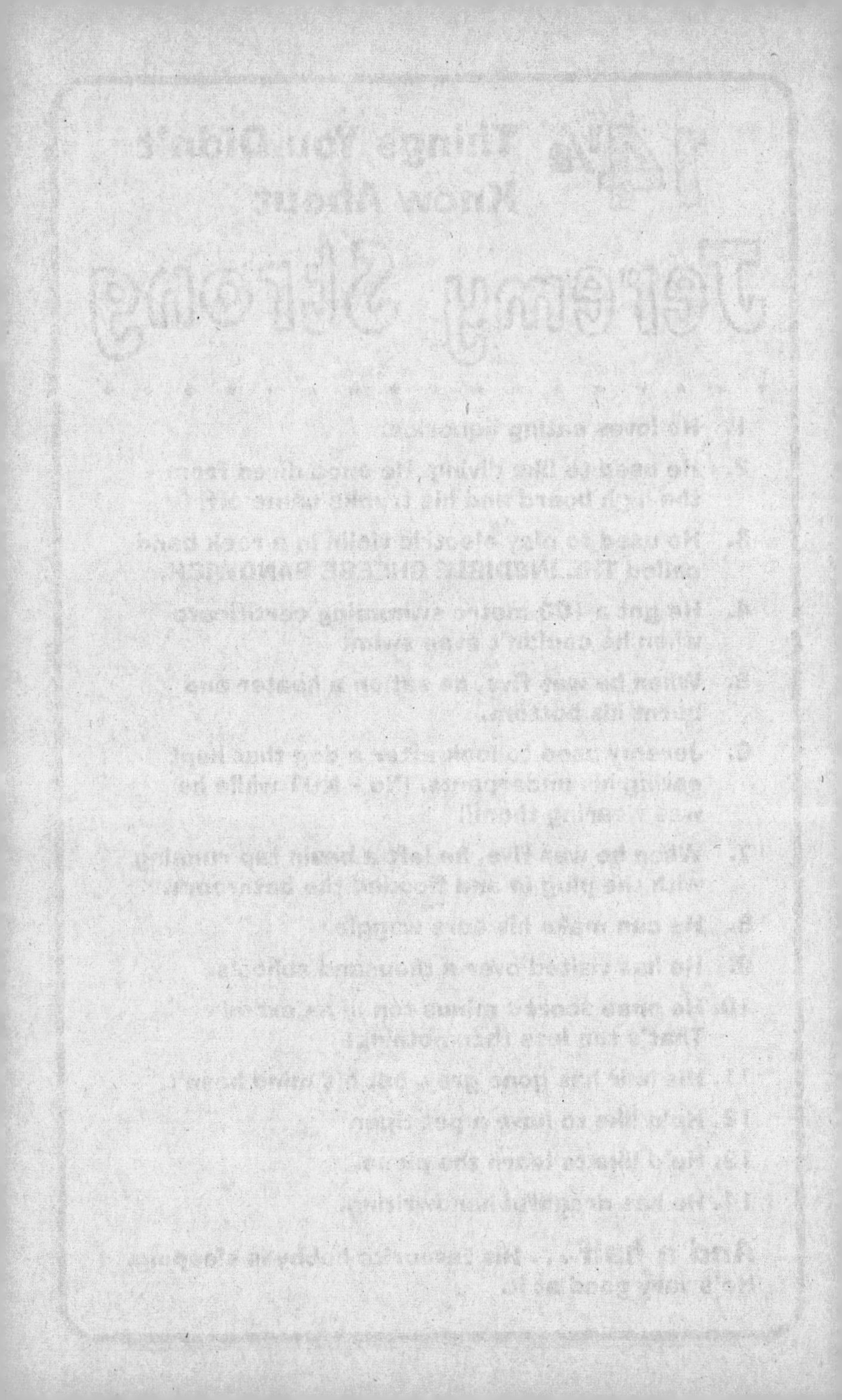

Of all the books you have written, which one is your favourite?

I loved writing both **KRAZY KOW SAVES THE WORLD – WELL, ALMOST** and **STUFF**, my first book for teenagers. Both these made me laugh out loud while I was writing and I was pleased with the overall result in each case. I also love writing the stories about Nicholas and his daft family – **MY DAD**, **MY MUM**, **MY BROTHER** and so on.

If you couldn't be a writer what would you be?

Well, I'd be pretty fed up for a start, because writing was the one thing I knew I wanted to do from the age of nine onward. But if I DID have to do something else, I would love to be either an accomplished pianist or an artist of some sort. Music and art have played a big part in my whole life and I would love to be involved in them in some way.

What's the best thing about writing stories?

Oh dear – so many things to say here! Getting paid for making things up is pretty high on the list! It's also something you do on your own, inside your own head – nobody can interfere with that. The only boss you have is yourself. And you are creating something that nobody else has made before you. I also love making my readers laugh and want to read more and more.

Did you ever have a nightmare teacher? (And who was your best ever?)

My nightmare at primary school was Mrs Chappell, long since dead. I knew her secret – she was not actually human. She was a Tyrannosaurus rex in disguise. She taught me for two years when I was in Y5 and Y6, and we didn't like each other at all. My best ever was when I was in Y3 and Y4. Her name was Miss Cox, and she was the one who first encouraged me to write stories. She was brilliant. Sadly, she is long dead too.

When you were a kid you used to play kiss-chase. Did you always do the chasing or did anyone ever chase you?!

I usually did the chasing, but when I got chased, I didn't bother to run very fast! Maybe I shouldn't admit to that! We didn't play kiss-chase at school – it was usually played during holidays. If we had tried playing it at school we would have been in serious trouble. Mind you, I seemed to spend most of my time in trouble of one sort or another, so maybe it wouldn't have mattered that much.

Want to keep laughing?
Enjoy even more hysterically funny adventures
from
Jeremy Strong
Laugh your socks off with Jeremy Strong
The Hundred-Mile-An-Hour Dog
Laugh your socks off with Jeremy Strong
Return of the Hundred Mile-An-Hour Dog
Laugh your socks off with Jeremy Strong
Krazy Kow Saves the World – Well, Almost
Laugh your socks off with Jeremy Strong
Chicken School
Laugh your socks off with Jeremy Strong
My Brother's Famous Bottom
Laugh your socks off with Jeremy Strong
My Mum's Going to Explode!
Laugh your socks off with Jeremy Strong
Beware! Killer Tomatoes
Laugh your socks off with Jeremy Strong
My Dad's got an Alligator!
Laugh your socks off with Jeremy Strong
My Granny's Great Escape
Out now!

Log on and laugh for hours!
Brand-new 100-mile-an-hour amusement at the KRAZY KLUB.
CRAVING MORE SILLINESS?
Join Jeremy's
KRAZY KLUB
at jeremystrong.co.uk
With hilarious new features:
Prove how KRAZY you are!
Addictive games!
Streaker's blog!
Plus:
Fab Competitions • Fun Stuff • Sneaky Previews
Interactive Polls • Hot Gossip
and lots more rib-tickling treats!

It all started with a Scarecrow.

Puffin is seventy years old.

Sounds ancient, doesn't it? But Puffin has never been so lively. We're always on the lookout for the next big idea, which is how it began all those years ago.

Penguin Books was a big idea from the mind of a man called Allen Lane, who in 1935 invented the quality paperback and changed the world. **And from great Penguins, great Puffins grew, changing the face of children's books forever.**

The first four Puffin Picture Books were hatched in 1940 and the first Puffin story book featured a man with broomstick arms called Worzel Gummidge. In 1967 Kaye Webb, Puffin Editor, started the Puffin Club, promising to **'make children into readers'**. She kept that promise and over 200,000 children became devoted Puffineers through their quarterly instalments of *Puffin Post*, which is now back for a new generation.

Many years from now, we hope you'll look back and remember Puffin with a smile. **No matter what your age or what you're into, there's a Puffin for everyone.** The possibilities are endless, but one thing is for sure: whether it's a picture book or a paperback, a sticker book or a hardback, **if it's got that little Puffin on it – it's bound to be good.**